Right On With Love

ZONDERVAN HEARTH BOOKS

Available from your Christian Bookseller

A HEARTH ROMANCE

Right On With Love

Lon Woodrum

ZONDERVAN
PUBLISHING HOUSE
OF THE ZONDERVAN CORPORATION | GRAND RAPIDS, MICHIGAN 49506

PROLOGUE

THE FUNERAL WAS a small, quiet affair.

The rank of mourners who followed the casket to the cemetery was thin; but the grief in some of them was as deep as the fog which clung to the Pennsylvania hills that Friday in September.

Neither CBS or NBC reported the funeral. It made the front page of *The Steel City Chronicle* only, I suppose, because the news media discovered importance in a violent death.

Wadsworth once wrote a poem about a girl called Lucy. Few knew she died, and fewer still cared. The poet, however, cried, ''But, oh, the difference to me!''

I think I know what the poet meant.

Most things that we experience dim fast in our memory. But I am certain there will ever come to me, as if on a taped play-back, the thing my friend used to say:

Right on with love, baby.

CHAPTER 1

My LOOK RESTED LIGHTLY on my wife, sitting at the breakfast table; and I thought of a caption I had seen in a well-known woman's magazine.

Can This Marriage Last?

Sally caught me looking at her and smiled. Sally always smiled easily. It seemed natural to her. Her red-gold hair was nicely arranged, as usual, her blue-green eyes deep. Sally was a lovely woman.

Why did I ever marry you, Sally? my mind said silently.

Taking my look from her I finished my coffee. Coming to my feet I said, "Take it easy."

She caught me at the door and kissed me. A tiresome ritual, as far as I was concerned.

"Have a nice day, dear," she said.

I grunted and went out to my white Buick convertible. Sally waved at me from the door.

Driving a few blocks I stopped in front of Spinoza Jones's "pad." He and I alternated weekly in furnishing downtown transportation. He was waiting on the sidewalk before his four-room place.

"Like it's an admirable day, friend," he said as he clambered in.

Apparently almost any day was an admirable day to him. At least I never knew him to lament an abominable one.

On my meeting him for the first time I had asked about his name. "One of your parents, or both, I presume, liked the philosopher, Baruch Spinoza, so they named you after him."

Spinoza grinned. "Can you believe a name like Horace, such as I was given at birth? Contemplate, if you can, the chagrin of a cat bearing such a cognomen through life. What was left but to name myself?"

"You, then, must like Spinoza's philosophy."

Spinoza wagged his head. "Not that he wasn't a cool thinker. It's like I dig the feel of the name. Like it hangs easy in my head."

Spinoza looked a little like Johnny Cash, only thinner-faced; and he was thinner all the way to the floor. He was smooth-shaven with rather long sideburns, and his blond hair came down to his collar in the back, but it was brushed back from his high forehead. He had eyes that were sometimes gray and sometimes blue, and now and then they were both. He always wore an odd assortment of clothes; you never knew what to expect in his raiment, except you knew he would never be wearing a necktie.

He was a top mechanic and worked for the same company I did, Acme Distributors. It seemed as if he would fit a guitar, but he couldn't sing. However, he had a voice deep as a Tennessee hound's. You thought of the South and of the West when you studied him, and rightly so; for he came from Dallas.

From what I had gathered his father was high in the world of the Establishment, and had made a great deal of money. Also, it seems, Spinoza and his father had struck the generation gap like two bull elks fighting over a cow.

Spinoza had taken to the road and gravitated toward the hippies of an earlier time. A slightly lame foot, the result of a fall from a horse as a boy, kept him out of the military service. So he became a wanderer with others his age in the mightiest and most affluent nation on earth.

"Like I walked with the unwashed," Spinoza had told me once. "Like I scrounged with then for provender, marched with them, smoked pot with them, went to jail with them. Came, then, one memorable evening when I attended one of Billy Graham's meetings to sneer and stayed to pray. The North Carolinian got through to me fast and hard!"

So Spinoza Jones had become a believer.

Often as the word "unique" is over-used, it was the word for Spinoza Jones. Flamboyant hippie; early American orator; Walt Whitman; angry crusader for righteousness; hard-headed realist—any of these might flit across your mind when you heard him express himself.

As we drove downtown this Monday morning Spinoza said, "It was not nice not seeing you in church yesterday, chum."

I grimaced a little. I never attended church. My wife did—she attended the same church as Spinoza. She attended every Sunday. Which I resented.

"How many Sundays does this make that I have missed?" I said with light mockery.

"Far be it from me to keep such books, friend. But doubtlessly such books are being kept."

After we had ridden in silence for a time Spinoza suddenly said, "Not every few minutes does one observe eyes with that particular color of blue."

"Eyes?" I said. "Whose?"

"Like those of your lovely frau," he answered. "Whose else?"

His words flustered me for a moment, but I said, "Nice to have a neighbor who likes your wife's eyes!"

Spinoza sighed deeply. "Fortunate indeed must be the cat who has found a right mate. It was said by a long-ago maxim-maker that whoever found a wife found a good thing.''

''In my opinion that maxim-maker should have said that whoever finds a *good* wife finds a good thing. Or maybe not so much a good wife as a *right* wife. But here's hoping you will find the perfect mate.''

What I said to myself was: I wouldn't be too adverse to letting you have *mine*, fellow!

Snapping on the radio I fished some news out of a sea of high-jumping songs. As usual the word from the media was of earth being caught in an agony that wouldn't let go.

Clucking off the radio I said, ''What's the world coming to, Spin?''

Never did I cease to be amazed at his instant and vigorous stance on any theme. ''The world will not, unquestionably, terminate with T.S. Eliot's whimper, friend. More likely it makes right on for cataclysmic judgment. *Upon the earth distress of nations, with perplexity . . . men's hearts failing them for fear, and for looking after those things which are coming upon the earth—*''

Knowing through experience that I had to get him off his eschatological steam-roller I cut in quickly,''More especially, how will it be with our own country?''

''Regarding this mighty Columbia, comrade, the far-out liberals grabbed the ball and ran clean out of the field into some other kind of game. The name of that game is permissiveness. Out goes all the old absolutes, and what have we left but a fat bag of questions? Like the great Book says, when the blind lead the blind everybody winds up in the void.''

''You always appear so certain of your conclusion—''

''Go into the crazy street, man! Like I've been there often, and you can smell the breeding anarchy. Does it require a genius to observe which way the wind blows? All the yak about peace and freedom—and which among them knows what peace and freedom mean, much less how to achieve it? So, as a certain scribe has said, we come to the end of our tether. Comes the deluge, then the great white stallion!''

"The great white—what?''

"The great white horse, and on him the mighty rightwing *fuhrer*. Clippity-clop, man, clippity-clop! The big cool cat with the political mystique and a bugle in his tongue—the charismatic reactionary thundering against the fat mess the liberals have made of things. And right behind him the gestapo and the black boots—clickity-clack! The iron wagons and the concentration camps, and the zeroing in on the special target, the terrified minorities—''

"Wait a minute!'' I cut in. "I don't buy all this.''

"Not you, comrade, not several million other people,'' snapped Spinoza. "Did not the gifted Santayana say, 'Those who will not remember the past are condemned to repeat it'? Have you observed how in our tormented time we try to jettison the past? Like we have all but forgotten that little cat with the little mustache who set the world afire and almost burned it down!''

"Nothing like that will ever happen again,'' I said.

"You and I, compatriot, never *did* see it. Like it happened when we were very young. But summon the spirits of those millions who perished at places like Dachau—ask them whether they remember!''

"Times have changed.''

"Allow me to come up with a quotation. Attend it: 'The streets of our country are in turmoil. The universities are filled with students rebelling and rioting. Communists are seeking to overthrow our country. Russia is threatening us with her might and the Republic is in danger. We need law and order. Without law and order our nation cannot survive. Elect us and we shall restore law and order.' ''

11

"Who said that—George Wallace?"

"Have you too jettisoned the past, friend? The thing is, the people *believed* what that voice said—the little cat with the little mustache!"

"Hitler said *that?*"

"Who else? In Hamburg. In 1932. Like they heard him and believed him and put him in power, and later, when they were clobbered by the black-booted gestapo they heard the little cat say, 'I am Germany!'

"Convince me, baby, that the masses will never again follow a madman into the void! Convince me that the nations will not follow the Antichrist to Armageddon, comrade!"

"Which reminds me," I cut in quickly, anxious to escape from his discussion of further eschatology, "are you a communist?"

"Like a cow likes a T-bone steak!" growled Spinoza.

"You seem plenty anti-fascist, and you use that word 'comrade' often—"

"Tell me, is it not a fine word? Shall I surrender it to the communists, and only because they are using it? Shall I, then, surrender such words as 'home' and 'love,' which the communists also use?"

By now we were parked behind the Acme Building; and I fled from Spinoza Jones's booming voice toward my office.

CHAPTER 2

My PLAIN-FACED SECRETARY, Charlene White, met me as I entered my office on the seventh floor of the Acme Building. She said, "Mr. Bengold has asked that you come to his office right away, Mr. Gann."

"Thank you, Miss White."

Immediately I sensed something eventful must be astir. You could not view as insignificant a special summons from Marvin Bengold, the president of Acme Distributors, Incorporated. Bengold was not the type to ask you in regarding trivial matters.

Adjusting my tie before the office mirror I was grateful that I had put on my most expensive dark suit that morning. My look lingered for a moment on the tanned-face image and the dark eyes under the thick dark hair. The image, I decided, reminded me somewhat of Tony Curtis!

Marilyn Hunter likes that face! I thought.

The thought sent something like an electrical charge running through me. Wouldn't it make any man feel rather taller in stature to realize that such a woman as Marilyn Hunter was a little crazy about him? It certainly would—if he knew Marilyn Hunter!

Marilyn Hunter was someone to think about—or to do more than that about!

Marvin Bengold's deep-carpeted office was large. So was

Marvin Bengold. Six-feet-two. Massive shoulders. You hardly needed to be an extensive student of human nature to sense that his craggy face had been built without too much concern for other people. He was the kind of individualist who, perhaps, has caused many people to reject individualism. Heavy gray brows jutted out over steel-gray eyes; his wide mouth was wrapped about an expensive cigar, which was unlit. The gray hair was carefully combed. Huge gold cuff links glittered beyond dark coat sleeves.

Bengold did a rather odd thing, for him, as I came in : he rose to his feet and said in a bass voice: "Good morning, Amos." Indicating a chair he said, "Take a seat."

He concentrated on me, his eyes narrowing; and I felt a certain inward disturbance. Bengold cleared his throat, took the unlighted cigar from his mouth and studied it for a moment. Then he said, "You have been with us quite a while, Amos."

I nodded. "Ten years, sir. Well eight years, really. I can't very well count those years in the military service."

Bengold lighted his cigar slowly with a gold-plated lighter. "Count those years, Amos. We always felt you belonged to us even when you were in Vietnam. We were sorry you were wounded; but that sent you back to us sooner."

"Thank you, sir."

Smoke wreathed about his face. "You were the kid out of nowhere when you came to us. We stuck you in somewhere—what department was it? No matter. I suppose none of us were in any sense expectant regarding your future. But you moved up pretty fast. You seemed to have a natural bent for moving stock. You got to be a field man. Now you are a department manager."

I nodded again, waited.

Bengold said, "You have done well, Amos. Really well."

"Thank you, " I repeated and waited some more.

He raised a big manicured hand. "Why don't we omit the 'mister' from our conversation? My name is Marvin. A few close friends call me Marv!" He chuckled as if he had made a joke. He appeared in a jovial mood. But my nerves tightened a bit more.

"I appreciate your work, Amos." He let go a mouthful of smoke. "The Board of Directors of Acme have been together for an unofficial discussion. That is, the majority of them have. By the way, have you heard that George Walden, our vice-president, will retire soon, due to failing health?"

"Well, I did hear something—" I replied.

"Probably you're not too acquainted with Walden. He's a good man, a credit to Acme. And I hate to see him step down from his seat. He has always had, not only a good head, a genuine loyalty for the company, but that particular kind of toughness that we need—no, that we have to *have*—in our top men! The fact is, George Walden will be a hard man to replace."

"I suppose so," I said in a low voice.

"As I said, some of us on the Board have been talking. We have been looking hard at a certain name. The name is Amos Gann!"

"You—you really mean—?"

"We make it a point to keep our eyes open regarding men we work with. We have watched you for some time now. We figure you for an authentic company man."

"I'm grateful," I said somewhat lamely.

"Understand, Amos, the Board hasn't spoken officially. But, as I said, some of us have talked. Things look real promising for you."

I almost said "I'm grateful" again but realized I was beginning to sound something like a parrot. While I fumbled for words Bengold frowned deeply, reached over to an ashtray and put down his cigar. "There is only one thing, Amos—"

He quit speaking, rose and went to a window which looked down on Steel City sprawling many stories below. He stood there for a time as if in deep thought. I could only wait for this next statement, agitated within. Finally he came around slowly, spearing me with a hard look.

"The vice-presidency is no small matter. And it pays a top salary, with a fine pension at retirement, to say nothing of other benefits that can result from holding such an office. I'm sure you follow me." He paused, then added, "Besides, vice-presidents have been known to become presidents!"

"I scarcely know what to say, Mr. Bengold."

The president of Acme Distributors hooked a leg over a corner of his wide mahogany desk. You could sense the pride of power soaring in him. "Of course, as I said, there has been no official decision as yet."

"A moment ago, sir, you said, 'Only one thing.' I was wondering what you meant."

His hesitation was slight before he said, "It's a delicate subject to bring up, Amos. Anything that concerns a man's private life is never an easy thing to discuss."

"My private life?"

He coughed lightly. "It's your wife, Amos."

"Sally?"

"When you come to the place where I stand—the place where *you* will be standing, if you become vice-president of Acme—one's private life becomes a tremendous factor as far as Acme is concerned. (Not in the old Victorian sense regarding prescribed social mores, of course.)

"When you are on a lower level, what you and your family are and do may not matter so much to the company. But when you stand at the top all that is changed. Everything you do is important to the company. Do you understand what I am saying, Amos?"

"Well, I trust I do, but—"

"None of us doubts that Sally is a good woman. She's attractive. In fact, she would fit into some places and be a mighty asset. And she would make some man a very fine companion—"

For the first time an anger stirred in me during the conversation. "Just what's wrong with Sally?" I demanded suddenly.

Bengold leaned forward, narrowing his look on me. "Maybe they call me ruthless because I prefer to put things to men without equivocation. So here it is. Sally just doesn't belong in our world!"

The inner anger escalating in me did not make me unaware that Bengold spoke the truth. It was not too difficult to read Bengold's thoughts. Just for one thing he was thinking of what had happened at some of our company banquets. Lately Sally had not been present at the company's goings-on. For me there had often been the humiliating question repeated by ranking company men, and more especially by their women: "Your wife isn't with you—?"

In the beginning of our marriage Sally had attended these sessions. But her dislike for the drinking, the risque jokes, and sundry other things, had turned her off. She ever appeared conscious of the fact these Babylonians of big business were strangers to her. Perhaps I should not merely say "big business," but rather refer to the special breed that made up the Acme world.

Remembrance of her words, spoken once after a special gathering where she was as out of place as a sunfish in a sandpit: "Amos, darling! I know you have to attend these things. And I know you will call me some sort of a snobbish prude—but these affairs leave me fairly ill. Actually, I fail to see what they have to do with business."

"There are probably a lot of things you fail to see regarding our setup," I retorted. "And if you feel like cutting out—"

"Oh, you know better than that. You know I'll go on—enduring everything, just for your sake. I'm your wife. But, it's impossible for me to *enjoy* them. Or, for that matter actually to enter into them."

We had discussed this thing, sometimes calmly, but more often heatedly. Once she said, "All that sham! It's like some command performance in some ancient kingdom with King Bengold being fawned over by his subjects, all anxious to show him how marvelous he is! Really, honey, the liege lords went out of style ages ago! I think the man is sick—sick from his love of power!"

"Come off it, Sally!" I cried. "You talk like a nitwit!"

"Take Marilyn Hunter," said Sally. "All that pretended sophistication! Her gush about Homer and Sappho—and then her telling her dirty jokes with utter charm!"

"Listen to me, Sally. Marilyn *is* sophisticated. She's a very intelligent person. She has poise; she knows how to handle people. Don't sell her short by talking about her pretended knowledge, either. She came from a big university with two degrees. Don't put her down."

Yet despite our differences, Sally was usually a perfectly sweet girl. You had to give her that. She was considerate; kindness seemed rather natural with her. The thought had often come to mind: she's cute as a kitten that needs a lap to curl up in!

She was tender enough at times to make a man hurt inside. Red-gold hair; slim; small-boned; full-mouthed: she was a lovely woman.

Sally. Country girl.

She belonged to Cedarville, a town with two drugstores. Only through some strange mismanagement of fortune had I ever seen her in the first place.

CHAPTER 3

I HAD GONE TO CEDARVILLE for Acme to consult a mining company. Sally had been in the front office working as a typist.

Unexpectedly, and unprepared, I had rammed head-first into a love affair. Just one of those crazy doings of fate.

While I was in Cedarville an inner voice kept nagging me all the time I took Sally out. And when I got back to Steel City the voice kept on as I was writing her. Something was warning me of the very thing which Marvin Bengold had brought up so bluntly: Sally was not of my world!

But who can argue with what we call love?

Sally herself, to be sure, was also troubled about the difference in our two worlds. But she, too, was in love. And love, finally, won the contest.

Phoning her from Steel City I said, "Darling, I'm coming to Cedarville." Which I did. And a few days later we were man and wife.

At first Sally seemed elated over living in Steel City in the eight-room house I had gotten for us. But it was soon evident how she stood in the pushy atmosphere where hard-headed and efficient women moved and made money and looked down with quiet scorn on those whom they directed.

Marvin Bengold's big voice broke into my thoughts.

"You have to be really tough in this world, Amos. We

have to be genuine realists. The junkyards of mankind are jammed with the dreamers and the idealists. You can see the kids storming about these days, dissenting, marching to Washington, howling against the Establishment. But these are mad winds that will blow themselves out. Finally only the pragmatic thinker will remain on his feet. Let me say it again: you have to be tough.''

He lighted another cigar, extended the box toward me. I shook my head. I didn't smoke cigars. The thought shot across my mind: maybe I *should* take up cigars—if I was going to walk in Marvin's world!

I said, ''What about Sally ? What are you suggesting I do about her?''

He bit off the end of the cigar carefully. Air whistled softly into his lungs.

''Were there the remotest hope of changing her—But we both know she's not the type to be reformed. And it's not just some social defection of her part. It goes a lot deeper than that. It's her *religion.*''

''Well, there's no denying she's religious—''

''I'm convinced, Amos, it's her chief trouble.''

I wasn't going to dispute that with him. Sally was never free from religion, anywhere, anytime. She probably had never been really free of it in her lifetime. She not only took it to church with her; she brought it home with her after church. She took it to a cocktail party. Especially she took it to a cocktail party!

Not that she had been an embarrassing psalm-singer at a pagan festival when she had attended our affairs. No spouting of Scripture; nothing of that sort. No over-pious attitudes. But everyone—somehow—recognized that she was a captive to religion! She smiled. She conversed in her modulated voice. But she was different from the rest of us. You could feel it. Everyone could.

Sally was a foreigner in our land. She was fitted for a prayer meeting! She was geared for sermons. For Bible passages, hymns, Sunday school picnics. To her we were the devotees of Moloch; her spirit was in a tabernacle somewhere with sheep not too far from the door!

Bengold had said it. She just wasn't of our world.

And we knew she never would be.

At the beginning of our marriage, because I wanted to please Sally, I had gone to church with her. I endured listening to a choir sing alien music and meaningless words into an ear that doted on Mozart and Chopin. I attended sermons by the minister at Calvary Church, Dr. John Blake, hearing him talk of old kings and old prophets, unable to apply their ancient goings-on and preachments to the history being made by space-age men. Sunday after Sunday I suffered attacks of *ennui*. Theology was a foreign country to me. I felt certain that religion was something invented for a breed far removed from my own.

Church picnics! Sally actually *liked* them! She was like a child. Again, to please her, I went; but each occasion was something of an ordeal. The people blatted away about things that meant nothing to me; they seemed obsessed with trivia. After each ordeal I discovered myself gulping two or three highballs—I who had always been a strictly one-drink-before-dinner man.

An old anger kept waking in me because I had failed to check more deeply into Sally's religious make-up prior to our wedding. Not that I hadn't found out that she was religious, for I had. In fact, I had even pretended to be somewhat religious myself, so enamored was I of her apparent innocence and her loveliness. Afterward, to be sure, I loathed myself for my pretension.

Looking back I could see that Sally's religion hadn't shown so well during the days of courtship as it did after we were man and wife. But it did come to show vividly until our married lives saw a bridgeless gulf, which religion widened, lying between us. Neither of us would, or could, cross it. I must confess that most of the quarreling over our views on faith, as far as words go, was on my part. But Sally's silent stand for what she believed was like a shout on her side sometimes! She was not nasty-tongued or outwardly bitter; but she was hurt by my unfaith. She tried hard to hide her wounds; but I always sensed them. The tension in our house grew.

Once Sally said to me, "I was a religious person, Amos, before I met you. But I was not really a Christian. But shortly after we were married I became a real Christian. I remember that I even tried to tell you about it, but you scarcely seemed to know, or care, what I was telling you."

"So what?" I muttered.

"Being Christian and being religious can be very different things," she said. "Had I been committed to the Lord when I met you I probably wouldn't have married you!"

How wonderful if you had been committed! I almost said aloud, but didn't. Aloud, I merely grunted.

Sally went on. "One thing I want to say, however. I married you because I loved you, Amos. And I want you to know something else."

"Like what?"

"I still love you very much!"

"Oh, for the love of—come off it, Sally!" I cried.

"I am telling you the truth, Amos. Before God! I don't even know *why* I love you—with things as they are between us. But I do. And at times that's all I really *do* know regarding us! In spite of all that has happened to us, I am still in love with you."

My mouth opened for some retort, but she added quickly, "But there is that other thing: I love God also! And all I know

22

to do is to stand on my love for both of you—you and my Lord!''

So, there we were.

We carried on like that. We endured our marriage. At least *I* endured my part of it. One thing: we quarreled less as time passed. The truth is, we *talked* less. Arriving at home in the evenings I grabbed a high-ball, drinking it alone, of course. We would have dinner. Then I would get alone with a book, preferably one of the latest novels, the kind of a book which Sally abhorred. Or I would read *Newsweek, Life,* or *Fortune*.

Sally was an avid reader, too. She read the Bible, of course; and any number of religious books; or a novel, if it wasn't too sex-loaded for her. Also she was strong on poetry, especially of the older school. She eschewed many of the modern bards, the *avant-garde* stuff.

When Sally and I carried on a conversation, now, we could do it without triggering a war—simply by not talking about anything in particular! We had practically come to a place of peace, a peace enforced by an absence of common feeling.

At mealtime I simply waited, with a sense of embarrassment, while Sally asked a blessing over the food. In the evening she retired first; I knew she would kneel by her bed and pray, so I felt it best that my pagan presence be removed! Prayer, to me, appeared a waste of time and effort. My pragmatic mind maintained that most of the things people prayed for might be obtained simply by going after them with gusto!

On Sundays Sally went to church and I remained at home watching *Face the Nation* and *Meet the Press* on TV. Or I worked over books from the office.

Memories of these things moved in my mind as I sat under the look of Marvin Bengold in his big office.

He said, "I repeat it. Religion, I think, is your wife's chief trouble."

I nodded, "I won't argue with you at that point."

"Isn't it only a matter of time until you marriage breaks up anyhow?"

I looked away from him, then back again. "You put it pretty bluntly. But you're probably right."

Bengold smiled bleakly. "Once it would have been considered bad in business for a top man to have a divorce. But things have changed—at least in some quarters. Now it is sometimes better for one of our big men to be divorced than for him to hang on to a wife who handicaps him in the business."

While I was trying to think of something to say to that Bengold added, "Have you ever considered how pleasant life might be for you if you had a wife with whom you were really compatible?"

I shrugged. "Naturally the thought has crossed my mind—"

"Say, for instance, that you were married to a woman like Marilyn Hunter!"

A flush must have appeared on my face. But Bengold laughed quietly. "It's all right, Amos. I've seen you looking at her at times!"

He was right, or course. I had looked at Marilyn many times and in ways that showed my feelings, I suppose. The fact is, I had often gone into her office just to be near her. At the conventions and parties we seemed naturally to gravitate together; and our repartees had usually brought laughter from the crowd.

Only yesterday Marilyn and I had been out to lunch and had a long talk. Marilyn was her usual captivating self, with her attractive clothes and lovely hairdo—and all that bright dark hair. And those gold-flecked deep-amber eyes. Eyes that clung to my face, steady, challenging, commanding. She lifted her tea-cup, watching me over its rim, and said softly, "To the future, Amos. To *both* our futures!"

I raised my hand in a sort of salute. "To both our futures, beautiful lady!"

"To paraphrase Shakespeare," murmured Marilyn, "something wonderful this way comes!"

"Oh!"

"It's in the air!"

"Is it, really?"

"Mr. Big is grooming you for something high in the empire of Acme! You just could be the king some day, dear! How about that!"

I shrugged my shoulders; but I smiled. "You are a bright, beautiful woman, Marilyn. But aren't you running a bit optimistically? I've always looked on you as a realist."

She set her cup down carefully. She laced her slim fingers together. "I'm a realist all right. But every woman, even a realist, I suppose, has a right to have a bit of romanticism stored away in her makeup. And even the most realistic man may not be free from romantic sensibilities."

"True in my case, surely. Else how did I ever turn out to be a married man?"

Her retort came swiftly. "So you know the dangers of romantic feelings!"

"Meaning—?"

"I refer to the fact, my dear, that you are *unhappily* married!"

Lifting my shoulders I let them down again. "I wouldn't try to laugh off that remark."

She reached and touched my hand quickly. "Whether it helps or not, I want you to know that I'm sorry about your unhappiness, Amos."

My fingers caught and tightened on her hand. "Believe

25

me, it helps. You know something? I'm not as unhappy now as I was before you said you were sorry I am unhappy!''

She let go a delicate laugh. ''But I also want you to know that I'm not *too* sorry you are unhappily married, darling! It would make me a lot more jealous if I knew you were genuinely happy!''

Yes. Bengold was right. I had looked a certain way at Marilyn Hunter.

Bengold's voice struck me again suddenly. ''Fortunately your marriage is not nailed down as tightly as it might be.''

I frowned. ''Not tied down?''

''I mean you have no children.''

His words thrust hard into me.

There had been a child. A son. Larry. He had been with us a year. That was probably the best year of our marriage. Larry somehow brought us together. I even enjoyed attending church to witness his christening.

But Larry only stayed with us that one year.

The bitterness that boiled in me at his funeral had never entirely left my heart. We had buried him on a bleak winter day; and the winter in my spirit was equal to the day.

This is it, my inner voice had shouted silently that day. This is it, for keeps. No more kids—ever. The gamble is too big. Never again will there be the risk of losing another Larry.

Sally, as grief-battered as I, but apparently without my bitterness, begged me to change my mind about not having any more children. She wanted, not one, but several more. She was not the type to be concerned too much with the population explosion!

''We have had a great tragedy, darling,'' she said. ''But we'll trust God not to let it happen again.''

''And He'll take care of it—like He took care of Larry, huh?''

"God allows such things to happen sometimes—it may be a test of our faith."

Wondering if Christians ever realized how their words sometimes sounded, I cried, "Let me tell you something. I'll only say it this one time. Then don't ever bring it up again. I'm not giving God a chance to test my faith twice!"

My outbursts wounded me, of course, almost as deeply as they did Sally. And I must confess that afterward it hurt me greatly to watch Sally looking warm-eyed at almost any baby that happened to be near her. Once I watched her lift a neighbor's baby to her heart, nestling her cheek against the infant's soft skin, and a knife-blade twisted in me. I turned away quickly to get the scene out of my vision. Tears fought to be felt in my eyes. But I hammered down my feelings. loathing myself for my sentimentality.

Snapping off the memory, I said to Marvin Bengold, "No children."

Bengold dropped down behind his mahogany desk and his look lifted to mine.

"One thing must be clear, Amos, even if I seem to repeat myself. The Board just doesn't want Sally in the setup. And *I* want her less than the rest of the Board!"

"You've made it quite clear!" I muttered.

"But the Board wants *you,* Amos. So do I."

A long breath expanded my chest. "You can mean but one thing regarding Sally."

"Yes. A divorce."

My look fell on my hands. My nails were well manicured. The look dropped to my shoes. They were good leather, and polished. I looked up and said, "Sally would never give me a divorce. It's against her religion."

"That will not afford a big problem."

"Reno?"

27

"People do it all the time. After all, you wouldn't mind a nice vacation, I suppose."

The man's attitude jarred me. Without willing it there arose in me a vast dislike of him. But I kept the feelings from making any parade. My mask fell swiftly into place. I was in the presence of a king. He was the spokesman for the parliament, the Board of Directors. The king had spoken. And I was a subject, at the king's mercy. Power looked out of his eyes. It sounded in his words.

Yet some inner agony made me put in a plea for mercy— mercy for Sally.

"She will be hurt," I said. "She will be awfully hurt."

A grim light stood in the king's eyes. "When you arrive at the top, Amos, you rather get used to seeing a few people hurt. That's how life is—even if hurting people never comes too easily. On the other hand it is never easy to *get* hurt. But if you want the high place you have to handle both. You have to hurt and get hurt. We are doers. The dreamers drop out. Only the tough can survive."

All at once I felt anything but tough. I felt nasty and mean; I felt as if I should have a bath. I could only stand there, unspeaking, wondering why I must be shamed in order to come to power. For I *was* ashamed. You can't throw someone out of your life to get gain for yourself without being ashamed. No matter if you have quit loving that one.

But Bengold was still speaking, his words hammering at me relentlessly. "Why should you prolong the agony? As I've said, it's but a matter of time before your marriage hits the rocks. You have admitted that. It will affect Sally deeply, of course. But you and I are aware that marriages are not made in heaven—wherever Sally thinks they are made! They are made on earth. And they often fail."

"Yes," I said. "They fail."

"Doubtless all I'm saying would sound calloused and

cynical to romantic souls. It would even sound harsh and brutal to the presidents of any number of companies. But Acme isn't just any company. It is Acme—and I am Marvin Bengold. Acme is big, and it will get bigger. We cannot afford to be stymied by the opinions of unsophisticated minds.''

Bengold took out a cigar and lit it; smoke curled about his craggy face. ''Acme needs men like you, Amos. You need a company like Acme. Ride with us and you will ride at the top of the world!'' He paused a moment, then said, ''And Sally will be right where she is now! Her own defections will bind her to her present place. If you want to go up where you belong you will have to leave her behind.''

I said, ''This thing is pretty unexpected on my part. I don't know just what to say—''

Bengold stretched out his hand. ''Don't try to tell me what you feel right now. Think it over. Slowly and carefully. Naturally I'll be eager to know your decision. Take the rest of the day off. Go somewhere and put your mind to it. Okay, Amos?''

CHAPTER 4

BACK IN MY OFFICE, dazed, I found my secretary looking questions at me when I told her I was leaving for the day. But she confined the questions to her look. Phoning Spinoza Jones I told him I wouldn't be able to give him a lift home.

"How pleasant to belong to the upward mobility class, so that one may wander off the job in the heat of the day," said Spinoza. "But many thanks for calling, compatriot."

As my Buick convertible thrust homeward through the traffic thoughts triggered a riot in my head. Uneasiness wrenched me as I imagined my confrontation with Sally. The word "divorce" had never been one of her words—except when she deprecated it.

Passing a steel mill stirred a playback from my memory-tape: a remembrance of back-wrenching hours spent at hard work in the steel mills.

My father had been a steel worker. I mean he *handled* the stuff. Handled it with big, hard hands. He was tough, an angry-looking man who seemed to revel in great physical effort.

It had been at my father's insistence that I had taken a job in the mills. But my stay there was brief. I had neither my parent's physical frame nor the disposition for such work. I recall saying to myself, "Amos Gann, you should rely on a thinking man's simple calisthenics to take care of your physical build-up!'' Selling steel, I decided, would be better than half-killing oneself wrestling with the stuff.

In a short while I was on the road for Acme Distributors. Salesmanship seemed rather a natural thing for me. Not that I had any intention of remaining a salesman.

Steel became a special study to me. While other salesmen were "living it up" in the evenings I struggled with hard-to-read books which gave me the lowdown on the commodity I was engaged in selling.

My diligence paid off. The word floated about that Amos Gann knew a lot about the steel business. The word even floated up to the top offices in the Acme Building in Steel City.

By the time I moved into an office in the Acme Building I had not only learned a lot about the business; I also learned a lot about the bigwigs who managed this particular business where my destiny was cast.

Acme, to be sure, wasn't in a common category with all the outfits in their world. Not all companies had their ruthlessness. But Acme was the crowd I was with; so I played the game by their rules. Well do I recall one of their chiefs saying to me at a gathering one night: ''We aren't influenced by all the old ideas and ideals that men have stuck up for people to go by. Ask me what is right and I'll tell you. What is good for Acme is right. What is wrong? What is bad for Acme.''

Rather than being repelled by their ways I was challenged. After all, in my thinking, man lived in a dog-eat-dog culture; so ignoring some of the old rules against trimming a few corners did not seem necessarily bad in itself. It was simply the way the game was played. And a man was an idiot to play to *lose!*

Now and then I found myself addressing Amos Gann in

this manner, "Sir, in a world like ours, a dog-eat-dog setup, what's wrong with being the top dog?"

Top-dog, then, it was for me. Whatever the cost. If Acme wanted a tough guy who was not handicapped by Victorian principles and mores, then I was that guy. From where I sat the old principles were open to suspicion, anyhow. The world at large was beginning to agree with that, wasn't it? Anyone could see how things were changing, including the attitudes toward man's behavior. Old ethics were becoming as sounding brass. After all, man was only a naked ape; what did you expect in an ape—an angel? Everything was up for grabs. What I wanted was a long reach.

Poor Sally! Country girl Sally. It was easy to envision the horror on her face should I really cut loose some day and tell her precisely how I felt about things! She would flinch as if from a redhot iron. She would see me as part of a monstrous world the Almighty had marked for judgment. But God, or the gods, and their judgments, as far as I was concerned, belonged to another time. God was not dead. He was just never born!

What a fool I had been to marry a woman like Sally!

What a fool Sally had been to marry a man like me!

I needed no gentle kitten for a mate! I needed a woman with a tough mind. Someone to prod the real giant in me and put me on the way to the highest.

A woman, say, like Marilyn Hunter!

Still, my memory-tape insisted on flicking off pieces of the past where Sally had played such a big part.

One scene: we were together on a picnic. It was six weeks following our wedding. Sally was wearing a white dress; she looked soft and sweet. And I felt a powerful masculine urge to look after her.

Our lunch finished, we faced a flaming sunset that screamed silently to be looked at. Sally's face was like a girl's; her red-gold hair gleamed. My throat tightened at the vision she made. For one fleeting instant I felt the desire to be *good*—as she was good!

Sally saw my look on her and suddenly she said in a half-whisper: "Amos! Always love me, will you?"

The tightness grew in my throat. I thrust my face hard against her bright hair and whispered, "I'll always love you, darling!"

It is quite possible, I think, that one never forgets moments like that.

Yet, now, threading through the traffic as I drove homeward after my visit to Bengold's office, it seemed impossible that this scene had ever taken place. It was like a long-ago dream.

What happens to people? What happens to a man and a woman whom fate has set down in a house to live together? That sweet sense of urgency that men call love—what is it? That wild, bright force that holds you like a fierce hope, then goes like drifting smoke-blobs?

You fight against that fate. You try to keep that love-thing alive. But you know you are losing the war. You sense how the war will come out.

What you did, Amos Gann, I said unspeaking, *was make a monstrous mistake! You fool! You got the wrong woman! It's that simple.*

Maybe the next time will be different.

The *next* time!

That was something to hope for, to reach after.

But that next-time hope would not, of course, erase the fact of how things were now. Certain things had happened to you whether you quite realized it or not. Ties had been made while you lived and breathed in a home with a woman, where you ate and laughed and slept together day after day and night after night. Bonds had been made that would not snap like rotten threads just because you willed it. The ties were iron. Old feelings hang on and old thoughts creep up out of deep places in the mind.

Marriage, cries some nagging voice, is made for keeps! How such an idea originated doesn't matter; it's still an idea difficult to shrug off.

My convertible passed a large church as I drove homeward later in the day and I said in silence, "Religion! Things might be different if Sally wasn't so hard-headedly religious! But what can I do about her? Like Bengold said: she won't change. She'll stick there where she is in her silly faith—even if it means losing everything else on earth. Religion makes such fools!

Religion has taken you out of my life.

CHAPTER 5

I TURNED MY BUICK into the drive of my eight-room blue-trimmed white house. Flower-smells teased my nose. It was spring; and Sally's flowers were celebrating the occasion. Once she had said to me, "Growing things are like little messages from the Lord."

The convertible eased into the two-car garage. Sally was wearing a bright blue apron and a concerned smile as I came through the back door. She put up her face for a kiss, even though she knew our kisses meant nothing any more. A Judas-feeling ran through me a I touched her soft cheek with my lips. I went hurriedly into the living room.

Sally followed me. "Are you all right, honey?"

She still used that term, which had become ridiculous. "Why?" I asked. "Why do you ask if I'm all right?"

"You seem troubled about something and you're home early."

I merely grunted and grabbed up *The Steel City* Chronicle. Sally gazed at me for a moment and returned to the kitchen.

I grunted again. I fixed myself a drink at the portable bar. The Scotch flamed in my throat; it moved like hot little lizards, running deep down inside me. I took another gulp and began fixing another drink.

It was going to be tough.

"Dinner will soon be ready," Sally called.

As if it made too much difference! Maybe I'd better have a third drink. I needed help. This rotten business had to be taken care of.

Thrusting my face before a living-room mirror I studied it. You're up there close to the top, man! I told the image. Hang in there and never let go. So someone gets hurt. So maybe *you* get hurt. Like Bengold said. Bengold is right, you know. He knows how things are in his world.

After looking at my face a bit longer I hurried to have that other drink.

During dinner my conversation with Sally was sparse. Once or twice I almost crashed through our quiet with blurting out what I soon must say. Yet I desisted.

After the meal I tried to become interested in a recent book about a man ruining his environment. But my mind refused to follow the print. Sally sat down with a book after she was done in the kitchen. I glanced at the title. *Moments With God.* How hopelessly caught up she was in that stuff!

Tossing aside the book I went into the den and switched on the color TV. A couple of ninnyhammers were screaming wretched jokes at each other. A commercial roared out at me, informing me that I would find it impossible to eat just one of someone's potato chips.

"Keep that first one, you idiots!" I said aloud and snapped off the set.

Moving back to the living room I found Sally still engrossed in *Moments With God.* Maybe it's best, I thought, that you are hog-tied to religion! Maybe religion is a good thing for those who must have something to fall back on when the going gets rough.

Suddenly setting my shoulders I crossed the room to Sally.

I said, "We have to have a talk, Sally."

She looked up from her book, a small smile blooming on her face. "What is it, Amos?"

My look ran away from hers. Then it came back. "Sally, I trust we can do this without a lot of emotion."

"Emotion—?" Her eyes asked questions.

My mouth tightened and felt dry. Then I came out with it. "Listen, Sally, I have to have a divorce!"

Her lips framed the one-word question, "Divorce!" But no sound came out of her.

A quick keen edge slashed at my insides. But I said, "Look. We're both adults. Grown up, I hope. Both of us realize that our marriage is a big joke. Why must we prolong the agony?" Then I loathed myself for not being original enough to keep from repeating what Marvin Bengold had told me.

"Divorce?" cried Sally, aloud this time. "What do you mean—Amos?"

"Look. You know what a divorce is."

"Why, it's—it's impossible!" cried Sally.

"Impossible? Thousands of people get divorces every day."

"But, Amos!" She stood stricken-eyed, pale. "Amos—I *love* you!"

"Love?" I frowned deeply.

Swinging away from her I went to the bar and did something I had never done before in my life. I drank a shot of Scotch straight, and I drank it after dinner. I set it down, coughing lightly at the fiery feel of it. I swung back toward Sally, repeating, "Love? Sally, you know better than that. You know as well as I do how we have been heading for this for a long time."

"No!" Her voice was something like a child's cry. "I've never believed this moment would come! Never!"

Glowering, my legs spread apart, I stood looking at her. "Don't tell me you've really been that blind, that stupid! That you haven't known how washed up we are! We have been washed up for a long time. A marriage like ours just doesn't make sense!"

"Oh, Amos—!" she whispered, and seemed to run out of words.

"We have become strangers in this house," I said. "We are foreigners to each other. We'll never be anything else. For decency's sake, Sally, let's break it off while we can at least remain friends."

"Friends?" Her head moved in a long negation.

Then abruptly she fled the living room for her bedroom. Fumbling for another drink I realized I was half drunk already. I slammed down the bottle and went to Sally's door. Beyond the door I heard her sobbing.

Scowling, feeling cornered and helpless, I stumbled back into the living room. I muttered to myself, "It's a rough thing, man. But you have to see it through."

All at once Sally stood in the doorway. Her tears had stopped.

"I prayed, Amos," she said simply.

"Well—" I waited, wondering.

"If you feel you must leave me, what can I do but let you go? I'm sorry I broke down."

"Oh, that's all right," I said lamely. "I'm sorry, too, about the way things have come apart—"

"I don't suppose it will do any good for me to repeat that I love you. It can't matter to you, I suppose, if you don't love me any more. But you know how I feel about a divorce, Amos."

I tried for a quick smile that didn't come off.

"You won't have to bother with it, Sally. Not in any way. I'll take a trip to Reno—"

"Reno?" The word appeared to jar her greatly. As though exhausted she dropped down on the davenport.

"It's the simplest way," I said. "I'll move out of the

40

house tonight into a hotel. And, speaking of the house, it will be yours, of course. You won't have to worry about things financially, either—"

Her head snapped up, tears were hot in her eyes again, but she kept them from overflowing. "Please, Amos! Let's not talk of money right now."

"All right," I said as gently as I could, although in the back of my mind I thought: it's like that with you romantic people. You never think of money when you think of love. But you'll think of money later—

My look ran over to the Scotch on the bar, but I didn't go for the drink I felt I needed. "It will be for the best, Sally. You'll see. You can still have a fine life. You're still young and lovely. You will find someone—"

She came up from the davenport, her eyes blazing. "Must you talk stupidly!"

Flinching, and thinking that women are hard creatures to understand, I muttered, "Okay, Sally. Okay. Don't get uptight."

"Uptight?" She put her hands to her face and spoke through her fingers. "Your world falls in on you without warning—and a man tells you not to get uptight!"

"Look," I muttered, "I'm going to pack a few things. I'll come for the rest of my stuff later."

In my bedroom I began shoving things into a suitcase. Any sense of victory I may have had was wallowing under a thick mattress of gloom.

Just as I was coming out of the bedroom a car rolled into the driveway. Sally went to the door and Rose Handor came in. Rose was Sally's mother. I stifled an inward groan.

"I was just driving by—" Rose said. She stopped, looking first at Sally's face, then at my suitcase.

Before I could think of anything to say Sally said, "He's leaving, Mama."

41

Rose, like her daughter, was a country woman. She had moved to Steel City after her husband's death to be near Sally. She said, "A trip—?"

"For good, Mama. He's leaving for good."

"We're getting a divorce," I explained bluntly.

Rose's head wagged. "You are joking, of course?"

"He's not joking," Sally said.

"But—children! You can't do a thing like this. You just can't—"

"Rose," I said, "will you let Sally and me manage our own affairs?"

Rose was a good-looking, gray-haired woman with eyes like Sally's. She had an intelligent face. She shook her head slowly. "It's incredible. I know you love each other—"

"Rose, we do *not* love each other!" I snapped.

But Sally cried, "I love *you!*"

"Let's not go into this again, Sally," I muttered. "You don't love me, not as a woman should love the man she must live with, day after day, night after night. Neither of us loves the other in that way."

Rose Handor caught a quick breath. "If you only knew, Amos, how many prayers I've prayed for you —"

Anger boiled suddenly in me. "Never mind reminding me how many prayers you've prayed for me! Or how many you've prayed for our marriage. I never asked for them. I don't *want* them, if you must have the truth. Can't you, or Sally, ever get it through your heads that I'm not interested in your religion or your God? Your religion is one of the major reasons why I'm headed for Reno. Can't you understand that?"

For the second time that night Sally fled out of my sight.

Rose faced me, her voice lifted a little. "You are making a tragic mistake, son. You are running out on love. And you are running out on God. Sally adores you. She needs you."

"She doesn't need me," I growled. "What Sally needs is some man who lives in her own world, who understands her kind of life. She thinks she loves me because—well, because by nature she is a *leaner*. When I'm out of the way she will find someone who will enjoy propping her up. And she'll love it! But, Rose, I'm just not the type of man for a prop!"

Her look on me was quite chilly. "I'm beginning to wonder just what kind of man you really are, Amos!"

My grin was bleak. "You've never really seen the real me, Rose. I've kept the guy masked! Better you never see him. You wouldn't like him, not one bit. I'm going to take him out of your presence before he lets his mask slip!"

Grabbing my suitcase I rushed for the door.

CHAPTER 6

IT WAS A LONG NIGHT, even if it was more than half gone when I checked in at the Palmer House. Sleep seemed like something I had never known. The room, although large, seemed narrow. I roamed about the place, my mind ragged from thinking.

Remembering the agony in Sally's eyes my mind was gouged relentlessly. However, ambition came to my aid, lending expectancy to ease the gouging. The thing I had reached hard for so long was almost at my fingertips. Power was about where my hand could close upon it. I was on the road up. And there was no road that led back to where I had been.

A line from a Shakespearean sonnet came to me and I said aloud, "Let me not to the marriage of true minds admit impediments." Ours would be a wedding of like minds—Marilyn's and mine. We had a world to make. It would be a big tough world, a hard world, but bright. And there would be music. *Our* kind of music.

I'm sorry, Sally, but that's the way it has to be.

The night was almost used up when sleep and I quit being strangers.

Fuzzy-headedness assaulted me the next morning when the desk rang my room. The happenings of the day before rushed into my mind like Marines on a beachhead. But by the time I bathed and shaved, my head was fairly clear again.

Just as I was entering the Acme Building I bumped into Spinoza Jones. He bestowed his usual grin on me and said, "Salutations and like that, friend."

"Hi, Spin," I said.

"Not observing your Buick at my pad," said Spinoza, "I buzzed your pad this morning. Your lovely frau appeared slightly more than uptight. Could it be, compeer, that you have domestic disturbances?"

I put a look on him and said, "Spin, shall I tell you something? You're one religious person I might tell about my personal affairs—"

He lifted a hand quickly. "Like speak freely, man, and without misgivings."

"Sally and I are getting a divorce."

Abruptly he was somber. "This, to me, is the saddest of news. Allow me, however, an observation?"

"The floor is yours."

"Like you scarcely appear one clobbered by fate."

"Well, Spin, I'll tell you. It's one of those things. It had to happen. It has been coming for a long time."

He nodded. "But it appears an odd world when *I* feel more sadness about your tragedy than *you* do!"

"Take it easy, Spin. Don't let my tragedy throw *you!*"

I didn't feel half as light-hearted as I sounded. Yet as I continued on my way to the office I began to marvel at how quickly I was departing from the responsibilities of wedlock. Perhaps the old life would fade faster and with far less pain than I had thought.

In my office, after glancing at some papers my secretary had left on my desk, I buzzed Marvin Bengold and asked if I might see him for a moment.

"Come right over, Amos," his gruff voice said quite pleasantly.

The usual cigar jutted from his mouth as I entered his office; smoke-fingers felt their way through the air. He waved me toward a seat.

"What's the word from you, Amos?"

"Well," I said, managing a thin smile, "at least my address is changed!"

"Oh?" he said behind a smoke-whorl.

"I'm staying at the Palmer House."

Bengold beamed around his cigar. "I like men of action."

"Thank you."

"So—it appears a vacation is in order. You remember what they say about Reno? The biggest little city in the world."

"Mr. Bengold—"

"The name is Marvin."

"Tell me—Marvin. The vacation in Reno won't be necessary before I know the action of the Board, will it?"

His head stirred negatively. "I don't think so. Just so we know you are making the arrangements."

"I see."

"I don't expect any arguments from the Board. My recommendation is on the table. The Board meets Thursday. Just relax and leave everything to me."

"All right." Suddenly it came to me that there was a sense of power just in being close to Marvin Bengold.

CHAPTER 7

THE GOLDEN PHEASANT RESTAURANT reflected the influence of an affluent patronage. You felt the effect of the subdued lights and the subdued music. The tablecloths were spotlessly white. The male waiters wore pale green jackets and bright smiles. Tall candles blazed at each table.

Marilyn Hunter wore a blue evening gown that went stunningly with her gleaming dark hair and dark eyes. The full mouth was bright with a smile.

"You're lovely, Marilyn," I murmured.

"Candlelight does things to one, sometimes," she said easily. "But thank you very much, Amos." Her look clung to mine through the candlelight.

"You scarcely look like a tough-minded business woman, sitting there like that."

She laughed lightly. "Nevertheless, I *am* a tough-minded business woman, my dear."

I sighed. "I'm wondering how you'd look in a kitchen."

"You, of course, are joking."

"Joking?"

"Kitchens are for cooks, darling. I am not a cook."

"Well, no—"

"Not that I look lightly upon the art of cooking. Someone has to do it. And some have become efficient at it. But kitchens are not—what is it the hippies say?—kitchens are

49

not my bag! Kitchens are for, shall we say, ladies such as Sally Gann!''

I winced a little, and Marilyn said quickly, ''I'm sorry, Amos. But since her name is mentioned—how is she?''

''She's not taking it in her stride, exactly.''

''She wouldn't.''

''She has phoned me several times at the hotel—''

''Naturally. When a woman is in love with a man—she *is* in love with you, right?''

''She keeps saying she is. She's a strange girl.''

''Almost any woman is strange to almost any man, in one way or another.''

''Perhaps we could talk about someone other than Sally,'' I suggested.

''Who do you have in mind?''

''How about Marilyn Hunter?''

''So? What about me?''

Reaching across the table I caught her hand in mine. She let me keep it. ''When this—thing—is over, Marilyn, I'm considering making you a proposition.''

''A job? Secretary to the vice-president of Acme Distributors? Dear, I have a much better job!''

''Even a business woman, I suppose, can be coy at times.''

''All right, Amos. We won't play games But a few things have to be taken care of before we can discuss what I think you're talking about.''

''Such as?''

''For one thing you are still a married man!''

''That will soon be no problem.''

''Another thing—'' She broke off, and a slight stain ran into her cheeks.

For a second I fought with a rising anger. ''You mean I'm not yet vice-president of Acme?''

Her blush turned to brass. "Mind reader!"

"Look. Are you interested in my position or in *me?*"

"Your position, my dear, will only reveal what sort of a man you are. Hence I'm quite interested in your position!"

I squelched my anger and grinned. "You're cute!"

She lifted her hand. "Call me ambitious, or sensible. Never cute."

"How about saying you're wonderful?"

"I'm still woman enough to like that! But, Amos, you and I are old enough to by-pass sentimentality. Love has to have a sensible foundation. Love, I rather think, is an authentic partnership. The kind of love that interests me, at least."

All at once, without willing it, I found myself contrasting Marilyn with Sally. I said, "I presume that you are still sentimental enough to believe in such a thing as home."

"To be sure. I want a home. I want a big, modern home."

"You're speaking of a *house!*" I said.

"A house is where a home is, darling!"

I gazed at her a moment. "Marilyn, let me pose a question."

"Why not?"

"Should a woman keep on working after she's married?"

She stared at me. "You ask that in the age of Women's Liberation?"

"You have a better answer than that!"

She seemed rather amused. "It all depends, I suppose, what sort of a woman you're talking about. Some women get married just to quit working."

"I'm not talking about just *any* woman."

"The answer is easy—if you're talking about me. Can you imagine my giving up all I've gained just to keep house? You can *hire* housekeepers, you know."

I thought: Sally and I never had a cook or a maid. Not

in all our years together. And there were years when we couldn't afford to hire cooks or maids!

But I nodded toward Marilyn. "Certainly two people can have a fine life together while they both make it in the business world."

She patted my hand. "It's nice to hear you say that."

CHAPTER 8

ON THURSDAY MARVIN BENGOLD called me again into his office.

"The Board meets this evening, Amos," he said.

"I trust all will be okay," I said.

"Rest easy. Nothing will come up which I can't handle."

That evening while the Board met Marilyn and I went out on the town.

After an extravagant dinner we hit several night spots. We laughed a lot and made wisecracks. We even sang a little.

At one point in the evening Marilyn said, "I think you and I are headed for real adventure together." She sipped her champagne, her eyes glowing darkly. "We'll live! We'll make money. Lots of money. We'll spend some of it. Keep some of it—"

She paused and I said, "What will we do with the rest of it?"

She gave a quick laugh. "Oh, I'll think of something!"

That night after leaving Marilyn I wandered about my hotel room. Questions jack-hammered my mind. What was Sally doing? Did Marilyn really love me? How would it feel to be vice-president of Acme Distributors?

Sleep showed up very late; and the next morning when my tired face looked at me out of the mirror I shaved it, noting the tiny lines running from my eyecorners, and I asked myself,

"What keeps you from sleeping, man? You're not yet thirty years of age and you're almost at the top."

My nerves were nagging me when my secretary said Bengold wanted to see me. En route to his office I ran into Marilyn. She caught my arm and squeezed it hard.

"Big day, darling!" she said.

In Bengold's office I felt a vast inner heaviness. It was as if I had suddenly thrust my head into darkness. It was one of those moments when you sense something that you cannot explain.

Marvin Bengold wore a somber face around his projecting cigar.

"Better have a seat, Amos," he said, unsmiling.

I eased into a chair, the dark feeling in me escalating. Bengold had the air of a high-priced funeral director. He let out a mouthful of smoke, said, "It's a funny world, Amos. A man has to be prepared for anything almost any time. You just never know—" He broke off, then said, "I didn't expect even a ripple." Again he stopped and stood looking at me.

In a choked voice I cried, "You don't mean—?" But my words hit deadend.

"I still find it incredible!" growled Bengold. "Bill Thompson! Bill Bower! These two pig-headed fools! But they *are* on the Board. How they managed it, I don't know. Oh, I'll find out, and when I do, let me tell you something—"

"I'm *out!*" I cried. Sickness began deep in me and rose fast. Sickness, and humiliation. And anger.

"They let me down, Amos. I mean, they let me down, hard. They tied my hands. The impossible happened."

"And this leaves me—where?" I said shakily.

Bengold slammed his cigar down on a tray. He came over and clapped his big hand on my shoulder. "The breaks can be tough, Amos. But don't let them throw you. It could be *I* overestimated my own power."

"But," I cried, *"I walked out on my wife!"*

He stepped back and examined me with his look. "One thing. You haven't gone to Reno yet."

"Reno? Man, do you think I could go back to her on my knees now and say, 'Please, I've made a big fat mistake? Will you please take me back?' I broke things off for good. Don't you realize that?"

He sucked air into his lungs. He ran a big hand over his chin.

"Amos, didn't you admit yourself that this break with Sally was inevitable, sooner or later? I certainly hope you will not blame *that* on me! So, what's happened between you and Sally is not the important thing. And, after all, it's not the end of the world. You haven't lost too much, really. It's not as if you're *fired,* you know. You still have a pretty fine job. You're still a big man with Acme. And who is to say that, given time, you won't ever be vice-president of the company?"

Embarrassed, sick, a climbing anger topping all other feelings, I thrust to my feet. "Is this really how this mighty Company operates? This stupid game with human lives? You ask a man to quit his wife—then you tell him you're sorry, but you can't come through with your end of the bargain."

Immediately Bengold's eyes frosted. "There's no sense in blowing up, Amos. Check this experience off as a lesson in the game. Like I told you once, if you can't take getting hurt you're not right for the game."

"Oh, I heard what you said! The trouble is, I *believed* what you said! I thought the mighty Marvin Bengold could deliver whatever he promised. Now, how do I ever believe anything you say? How do I know I won't be *demoted* in a few days? The way the game is played!"

"Listen," snapped Bengold. "Don't be so self-righteous! Are you really mad because you left your wife as much as you're not becoming vice-president of Acme? You seemed very willing to play the game until you drew a bad hand; now you want to rave like a spoiled kid and ask for your money back!"

"Bengold, I've never been so sick of anything as I am over Acme right now!"

Bengold seemed to grow over-calm. He lit a cigar slowly while I fumed. Then he said, "Amos, could it be that the Board was right in not elevating you to the office of the vice-presidency? The way you are carring on—"

"Why, you two-bit Nero!" I shouted.

"Gann!" His voice crackled. "You've said too much. I know you're over-wrought, but don't push too hard!"

"Now you open up with threats—"

"I have fired men—"

"Oh, you have, have you? Well, You'll never fire me, Mr. Big. I just quit!"

CHAPTER **9**

PLUNGING BLINDLY to my office I began throwing things together for leaving when Marilyn suddenly stood in the doorway. She came in and shut the door.

"Well, Mr. Vice-president, how does it—?" The look on my face stopped her. "Amos! What on earth—?"

"Cancel all congrats, honey," I gritted. "I'm not Mr. Vice-president. In fact, I'm no longer in this office!"

"What are you saying, Amos?"

"The deal washed up. I blew my top. I'm not only not vice-president, I'm out of a job. Period."

"You're not *fired?* You can't mean that."

"Oh, can't I? Well, maybe not fired. I quit. I'm out."

"That's impossible!"

"You think so?" I caught her by the arm and held it tightly. "Look, darling. Let's get out of this rat's nest! Let's go somewhere—and find a decent world!"

"Decent world?" She stiffened visibly and took her arm from my grip. Her mouth tightened. "Will you calm down, Amos? Think what you're doing. How long do you suppose it would take you to get to where you are in any other company?"

"Don't you understand that I am *nowhere* with this company? I'm through with Acme. I'm finished. Forever!"

She shut her eyes like someone in prayer—but I know that wasn't what she was doing. I grabbed her arm again. "Let's walk out of here, Marilyn. Let's go make a beautiful life, somewhere!"

She achieved a thin smile, thin and cool. "Go get a drink, Amos. Cool off. I'll talk to Marvin. Later I'll talk to you. Okay?"

"Listen to me, Marilyn—"

She frowned. "Don't argue. You're not in your right mind. We'll talk later. Right now I have a job to think about. *I'm* still working, you know!"

She swung around abruptly and left.

I jammed stuff into my briefcase furiously. Bengold did not buzz me. The king would not stoop to a dissenting subject.

Out on the street I headed immediately for a bar. When I ordered a drink the bartender said, "Something wrong, Mac?"

"Mind your own business!" I retorted. "I'll look after mine. Okay?"

"Okay," said the bartender. "Well, *okay!*"

Two drinks sank in my stomach, one right on top of another. Getting into my convertible I drove to The Palmer House.

But the room seemed to suffocate me. I felt trapped. For one wild instant I had the urge to drive home to Sally.

But I killed the urge.

With cooling rage I realized just what I had done to myself. I had lost both a wife and a job. And in such a brief time!

Later I phoned Marilyn and asked her to meet me at Gino's, an exclusive spot on Fourth Street. She agreed.

In a booth at Gino's I was working fast on a third Scotch when Marilyn appeared. She seemed quite perturbed.

She sat down, ordered a drink, and said, "Amos, I'm worried sick about you!"

"Oh?"

"I'm especially worried since I've talked to Marvin Bengold. I found him adamant."

58

"You talked to him—about *me?*"

"About you—who else? I tried to defend you. I told him you would be all right after you cooled off. But the trouble was, *he* wasn't cooled off! He told me to forget you! I'll speak to him again tomorrow—"

"Oh, will you come off it, Marilyn? Who asked you to intercede for me with that louse?"

She stiffened. But she sipped her drink almost daintily. Then her head turned negatively. "I'm more sorry for you than I can say, Amos. But I must have been wrong about you!"

"Just what is that supposed to mean?"

"Perhaps it was a good thing the Board rejected you! The way you are acting—"

"That," I shouted, "is a direct quote from the great louse, Marvin Bengold!"

She flinched, then said, "Amos, are you open to advice?"

"Advice?" From whom?"

"From me. Things are not going to be easy with you after what has happened today. You're going to need help. You'll need someone to stand by you—someone who will love you, no matter what. Why don't you go back to Sally?"

While I gaped at her she added, "Sally will forgive you for what you've done to her and take you back. She's a *Christian*—remember?"

The mockery in her voice was inescapable. A blade of hot pain sliced through me.

"It's a hard thing to believe," I muttered bitterly. "That you are the same woman I have desired for a long time! A woman that I wanted to offer a wedding ring! But you are a stranger! You never did see me as a man! You were looking at the future vice-president of Acme Distributors! How could I have been such an idiot?"

Her face was set. "Must we make things worse than they are? Get hold of yourself, Amos!"

Fury suddenly rocked me from head to foot. I upset my drink surging to me feet.

"A female Judas! So help me! Well, why don't you get back to your rat's nest? You belong there!"

What else I said I do not remember. I stood, shaking with wrath, watching her stiff back as she departed from Gino's.

My head wagged while deepening gloom wrapped me up slowly. Now I had not only lost a wife and a job.

I had also lost a girl friend!

CHAPTER 10

G̲ROPING MY WAY to the bar in Gino's I located a stool and boarded it.

"Scotch—double!" I almost shouted.

The bartender eyed me coldly. "This is a respectable place, sir. I think you have had enough to drink. How about a walk?"

So I started on a long, dark road—with a bartender telling me that I was an unfit patron. But I was too spent to argue with him. I wobbled off the stool and headed for the street. En route to the Palmer House I found another place which was not so particular about the condition of their patrons so I had another double-Scotch.

But I was too restless to sit and get drunk. I found my Buick and went for a drive, unconcerned too much with where I went. Wherever I went it was like driving into an empty future. The lonely, long road of a salesman began unwinding in my imagination and I shuddered. I had been on that long trek to that nice office high up in the Acme Building. It made me half-sick to remember.

Yet what else remained for me? With no letter of recommendation from Acme Distributors for whom I had given so many years, where would I find a place remotely equal to the one I had jettisoned in anger?

Engulfed in thought I had driven far out of Steel City

without realizing it. My foot lay heavy on the accelerator as if glued there. My speed was far in excess of the limit. The convertible swung around a long curve and began slipping from my control. The wheels howled on the pavement. Then I was off the highway and plowing through a field of under-brush. The Buick slammed hard against a large tree; my head cracked against the windshield. And darkness came down on me.

Faintly from afar I heard the thin sound of a siren. Then there were excited voices about me. When full awareness returned to me I was in a hospital room. A nurse loomed over me, and a man beside her who turned out to be a doctor.

My hand groped upward and I discovered a bandage on my head. The crackup of the Buick came back to me.

How about that? I thought dazedly. Now I have lost a wife, a job, a girl friend, and a car!

"Not much left," I muttered.

"What's that?" said the doctor.

"You wouldn't be concerned about it," I said.

The doctor smiled. "I'll say one thing. You're a very lucky man. Not even a concussion. You'll be back on the job in a few days."

You want to bet? I said silently.

He said, "You should thank Whoever looks after people who drive like mad when they're a bit full of the grape!"

"Scotch," I growled.

"It all works the same behind the wheel," he said.

I slept a while after that. Then the nurse woke me and said, "Someone to see you, Mr. Gann."

Sally was standing there, then. Dropping by the bed, close to tears, she cried, "I heard it on the newscast—"

I almost caught her to me and said, "Who on earth is like you, honey?" Instead I shut my eyes tightly. I said grimly, "You shouldn't have come."

"With you *hurt?*" she said. "I had to, Amos."

With the voice in me crying for her to stay there was but one thing to do: drive her away! I won't bore you with trying to explain it. Maybe you can't explain it. I turned my head from her and said, "This stupid accident hasn't changed anything, Sally."

She was silent for a moment. Praying, I suppose. Then she got to her feet. "You're right, I suppose. I'm only grateful to God you weren't hurt more badly. Forgive me for bothering you." She fought against tears and added, "I will be praying for you."

Then she was gone. And I lay there, angry at her for promising to pray for me. Angry at Marvin Bengold. Angry at Marilyn. Angry at everyone I could think to be angry at. But mostly angry at myself.

Later another visitor was in the room.

"Like, man, you hear about accidents these days almost before they happen," said Spinoza Jones.

"Hi," I said.

"It is to be hoped you are not banged up more than a little. How any of us survives the emergence of the automobile is a vast mystery."

"Nice of you to come, Spin. The Doc says I will be out in a few days."

He put a penetrating look on me. "Things happen. Some of them are sad. Like getting clobbered in a car wreck. Or like losing your position with a big outfit like Acme."

"So you've heard."

"Things get around, friend."

"So they do, friend."

"The possibility is, comrade, that you do not solicit my sympathy, but I extend it nonetheless. Furthermore, and, again, I may be operating minus your wishes, I shall be putting in a few of my sincerest prayers for you. Like the great Book says, we ought always to pray for everybody."

"Which makes two of you!" I muttered.

"It could be I am not reading you, chum."

"Sally was here. She's praying for me, too."

Spinoza nodded. "She would be, unquestionably. She is an authentic believer. I was aware before I came that she was praying for you."

"Aware?"

"Like I went to see her right after I heard of your breakup."

"Oh? Nice of you."

"Was I not obligated to visit a sister in distress? And the sister's distress was no small affair. Like she's in love with you, man!"

I took in a long breath. "Spin," I said, "I rather like you. Help me to keep liking you by letting me handle my own domestic affairs. How about it?"

Spinoza beamed a grin at me. "Far be it from me, friend, to interfere in the marital squabbles of the unhappily married. Yet, undeniably, it is my duty to assuage all the human agony that I possibly can."

"Okay. Okay," I grumbled.

"The chances are, friend, I am sent to leave you a thing to think on. All these things that appear to be against you may be otherwise in reality. Like maybe the good Lord is clobbering you somewhat to bring you to that point where you have a truer perspective on things!"

"It could be," I snorted, "that you are sticking your nose into things not your business!"

"Like I attempt to do two things: inform people of the way, and *show* them the way! Did not the great Martin Luther say like this: put hands and feet to your prayers?"

Then he was gone before I could muster an irritated retort.

CHAPTER 11

LIFTING A CUMBERSOME CRATE I set it down on top of another crate. Little sweat-creeks ran down my face. Tiredness nagged my back and knees. Pausing a moment I looked about the huge warehouse where I was working.

So here you are! I said to myself bitterly.

I wiped sweat from my face with a dirty handkerchief. Had it been only a year since I stood in Marvin Bengold's office and heard him tell me that I might become the vice-president of Acme Distributors?

Through bitter memory the days flashed back to me that I had spent knocking on office doors, attending interviews, and—having no recommendation to present—going back through those same doors empty-handed and heavy-hearted.

Finally it hit me that only the sales road was left open to me. Finding the first job in that field had not been too difficult. The Ringer Company had taken me on; and for a few weeks things had not been too bad. But my heart just wasn't in this sort of thing. You don't walk down from up there at the pinnacle and start slogging at the bottom without something happening to you.

Day after day the inner agony wore me down. Night after night it wore me down some more. That brain-stealing institution of modern man, the bar, became my refuge. I parked there until late in the evenings, swigging my tomorrows out of a glass. It even got so that after my appointments in the morning I would spend a hour or so with the booze at noontime. Although I wasn't quite drunk in the afternoons, the attitude of my clients began to change. This frustrated me further until by evening I was really ready for the bars again.

My sales began slipping badly. So much, in fact, that the Ringer Company notified me I was through. They did it rather politely. But I was certain what they were saying when I was gone. A real stumble-bum, that one, huh?

After a time I found another job with a company smaller than Ringer's. I gave myself a number of lectures. This time you have to make it, Gann! Time takes no vacation, it keeps going. And you're not moving with it. In fact, you are standing still. No, you're not even doing that—you're going backward!

The new job lasted six weeks.

Then the fact rammed hard into my hung-over head one morning that I just wasn't fit to be a salesman any longer! A sudden fear of booze kept me away from the bar for several days. But a devastating sense of loneliness and frustration finally drove me back to the taverns.

With my last sales job gone down the drain I tried drinking myself into forgetting about my tough luck. But, sobering up, the tough luck was still with me, plus a murderous hang-over.

Eventually I was here in this warehouse, a laborer, handling big crates of stuff.

Right now I stood in the big warehouse, my head moving as if I was saying "no" to someone. I was thinking: *Remember when you were going to sit up there on the top floor of the Acme Building? How you were going to live with that incredible charmer, Marilyn Hunter? How the mighty man has fallen flat on his face!*

A hoarse voice sounded in my ears. "For this we put out

American money? To pay a man to stand around and have a nice day dream?"

Wheeling, I saw the warehouse superintendent glowering at me from under shaggy brows. It was enough to make a man laugh—Amos Gann being bawled out by an uncultured guy who, a few months ago, would have practically lifted his hat in Gann's presence!

But I didn't laugh. What I did was stoop down and lift another crate. An argument would only have sent me to the paymaster. Apparently my particular job hadn't even led the union to organize it!

Quitting time found me stumbling out of the loathsome warehouse, feet-dragging tired. En route to the rooming house where I stayed a tavern crossed my path and swallowed me up. This was routine for me now. The bars were becoming more and more important to me.

While putting away three whiskies in quick order I looked at the bottles of expensive Scotch on the shelf and remembered how I used to look askance at the man who drank anything but high-priced Scotch. Then I shrugged. Even the cheaper bar whiskey was costing me almost as much as I spent for room and board.

Back on the street, headed for the rooming-house, I ran into a crowd of young people waving banners and shouting against the war in Vietnam. Some of them were shouting against the Establishment in general. The males in the crowd would soon be old enough for the military draft.

Suddenly a hand touched my shoulder and a familiar voice boomed in my ear. "Is it possible, friend, you have thoughts of joining these idealistic young citizens?"

Turning to meet Spinoza Jones's grin, I said, "They probably wouldn't care to consort with a square like me."

"However, considering all that has fallen you, compatriot, do you class yourself as a part of the Establishment?"

67

A flush crept across my face. "You have to rub it in, huh? Frankly, none of these kids loathe the Establishment as much as I do, I'm sure. I have more reason to hate it than they have."

"Irrefragably," agreed Spinzoa. His look ran over my stained working clothes, my unshaven face. Too, he was doubtless getting a smell of the booze on my breath. "The Establishment might well bug you no end."

"You'd better believe it," I said.

"You have been considerably on my mind of late, compeer."

"Oh, is that so—comrade!"

"You, and your lovely frau."

I frowned. "You feel quite some concern for my wife most of the time, I take it." Irritation scratched me.

"Such a woman would be worthy of any man's concern, chum. But, as you are aware, she and I share a common faith."

"Yeh, I know. You are both dyed-in-the wool believers."

"That—and we are very good friends. Nothing more, I assure you."

"Has anyone accused you of being anything more?" I snapped. "And what if there *were* something more? What business is it of mine? The truth is, you may be just right for each other! Both about the same age. Both idealists. And both hooked on religion!"

"Hang on to your cool, comrade!" chuckled Spinoza. "Allow me to pose a question which troubles my mind. Like how can a cat with your intelligence have lived so long with a doll without knowing something about her?"

The old anger that Spinoza always seemed capable of stirring up was back. "How many times do I have to ask you to let me attend to my own affairs?"

He waved his hand. "So be it, friend. Why do you not

accompany me to my pad and we will talk over sundry things."

I shook my head, angry at myself because I wasn't angrier at Spinoza. "Forget it." I moved away, turned. "Maybe some other time." I left him standing in the streets gazing after me.

I also heard him say, "Dominus vobiscum, baby."

My key was rattling in the door of my room when Anne Macey stepped outside her room across the hall. She had managed to be doing that on several occasions lately.

"Hi," she said.

"Hi," I answered.

She wasn't a bad-looking woman. In fact she was somewhat attractive. Tall, red-haired. Always smiling. She wore her expensive clothes well. She also had a bold look.

"Hard day?" she asked.

"They're all hard. Every lousy one of them."

"Want to step in for a drink? I've got to run on an errand, but I have time for a quick one."

I almost nodded I did want a drink. In fact I was figuring on having one in my room in the next few minutes. But I shook my head at Anne. "Not this time. I'm sick." I winced at my lie.

I didn't want to get tangled up with Anne. Or with any woman, for that matter.

"Oh, I'm sorry," Anne said. "Can I do anything?"

"Nothing. Thanks. I'll be okay."

Hurrying inside I grabbed the bottle for a quick drink. I looked at myself in the mirror. Maybe you didn't lie. I told the reflection. Maybe you are pretty sick!

It was mealtime, but my appetite was small. Food scarcely seemed important to me these days. Peeping out, and assured Anne was gone, I returned to the street.

A brief walk and a bar glittered across my path. Bars

always managed to do that for me. I went in like some forest-thing seeking shelter in a cave. In my deeper mind I was aware that each bar-visit was a brief stop on a dead-end street. But the street ran the way I happened to be going.

After a few drinks I was back in the streets again. Somehow, I felt I had to keep moving. I must have walked a long distance, for all at once I realized I was in front of the Golden Pheasant Restaurant.

This is the place where you dined with the charming Miss Hunter! I told myself.

Then, of all coincidences, who should be standing right there on the sidewalk but Marilyn Hunter herself.

Marilyn Hunter. Dressed like the Princess Grace. Carrying herself like a princess. And who should be with her but a king! King Marvin.

The king held the arm of the princess. They were both laughing over something he had said. They approached the restaurant entrance, never noticing me.

A tormenting rage began deep and rose fast in me, backed by memories that never slept too soundly in my mind. Anger, and the booze inside me, allied themselves together for action. I blocked the path of the king and the princess.

"Greetings, my gracious friends!" The bitterness in me put an edge to the words of mockery.

Marvin Bengold stared hard at me. He was about to brush me off as some intruding bum; but he leaned forward and began shaking his head.

"For the love of—can it really be?"

"Oh, yes, Marv, old buddy, it can really be!" I jeered.

"Amos!" cried Marilyn. Then again, "Amos!"

Bowing mockingly toward her I said, "So nice to see you remember me, darling!"

Bengold caught her arm and started to push her past me

70

without further words. But I blocked his move.

"Have a hard look at me, Marv!" I gritted. "How'd you like me for a vice-president? I'm qualified, you know. I'm a free man. Whatever entanglements, domestically speaking, which I once had—!"

"Please!" said Marilyn coldly. "Must we make a scene in the street?"

Whirling toward her I cried, "Haven't you heard? That's where they're making the big scenes against the Establishment. Right in the streets! People like you and Marv here— you've turned the kids into the streets with all those howling obscenities. Some of 'em with fire! Do you realize—"

Angrily Bengold reached out and pushed me back hard. "Get away from us, Gann! And get away *now!*"

"The big, tough king!" I said. "Old hard-faced Marv."

"You're drunk!"

"Oh, yes. Drunk. But even drunk I've been lying awake nights thinking how nice it would be to do just one thing. *This!*"

My fist smashed squarely into his broad face. He grunted and stumbled backward, almost going down. Marilyn screamed in my ear. I followed up and slammed him again in the mouth. Blood spurted; and this time he went down to his knees. Marilyn was still screaming. I swung toward her and cried, "How do you like this pig down here on his knees in the dirt, where he belongs?"

Bengold was up again in a moment, and I hit him again, hard; this time he stretched out on the sidewalk and lay groaning.

A hard hand dragged me back and banged me fiercely against the wall. I found myself looking at a uniform. And at a badge.

"What's eating you, Mac?" growled the cop.

The rage and the booze in me were still eager for a

beachhead. "Enter the fuzz! The mighty fuzz! The Establishment is saved!"

"Put your hands behind your back!" the cop ordered.

By then another policeman had arrived. My hands were manacled behind me.

"Right on with the revolution!" I shouted.

Marilyn was crying. "Phone for an ambulance, please. Someone. This man is badly hurt."

"You know something?" I cried to her. "That man once told me you had to be able to get hurt if you wanted to stand at the top!"

"Come on, fellow," said one cop. "Let's take a ride downtown."

A bleak laugh came out of me. "I always wanted to ride in a fuzz-wagon. Will you turn on the siren? I love to hear 'em howl!"

CHAPTER **12**

YOU HAVE TO BE INSIDE a jail to really know about one. Visiting one doesn't tell you too much. Jail is something you have to *feel*. Something you have to smell. You have to be there a while before it comes through to you what a jail is. And when it does the realization can be pretty frightening.

Hunkered on my hard bunk I listened to the jail-sounds floating around me. Jail-jargon. Bitter. Obscene. Angry. Vicious. Cages full of human beings, their minds all zeroed into one thought: freedom.

A month had dragged by since I began my sentence. Five months yet to go!

There had been, of course, no trial in my case. The case was utterly one-sided. Openly, before a number of witnesses, I had attacked a man on the sidewalk, hammering him into unconsciousness. I was a nobody; my victim was one of the most powerful citizens of Steel City. Entering a plea of guilty I had waited for the judge to do his thing. The judge was a fine-looking fellow with low-key rhetoric. He was cool, and sounded kind even when he said, "Six months." Being a judge must be a tough assignment.

A month finished. Thirty days. Seven hundred and twenty hours.

Marvin Bengold was back at his big office high in the Acme Building, all healed nicely from my assault. Maybe he had all but forgotten the assault. What had passed in Marilyn's mind after the incident? *(Just think: I had even thought of marrying that madman!)*

The papers made quite a thing of the happening, of course, Marvin Bengold being who he was—and the fact that I had once been a big man with the Company. But the press had soon run out of anything further to say about the incident.

This is a strange world—even when you are in jail. One day they shoved a man into the cell next to mine; and after the door rattled shut I heard a voice come booming from the newly occupied cell.

"Baby, it's like you never surmise what may be next on life's agenda!"

I almost shouted: "Spinoza Jones!"

"Incontestably, friend," said Spinoza. "And, inasmuch as fortune has flung us together in such an amazing manner, let me first apprise you of the fact that I came down here to this hoosegow to see you directly after you were incarcerated. But the fuzz politely informed me that my business with you was not of the utmost importance. Plans were formulating in my mind for another assault on the bastion gates when—incredible as it appears—fortune fixed it so I could have a nice visit with you. Like it's an unpredictable world, chum!"

Making a negative head-motion I said, "I don't get it. What are *you* doing in jail? Don't tell me you stuck up the First National, or something."

"May I be pardoned, friend, if I represent myself as a paragon of law-and-order citizenry?" said Spinoza. "This, to be sure, was not always true of me. Once I was a very angry rebel, and was betimes clobbered by the opposition. Unassailably, like most of the clamoring dissenters, I was a revolutionary without plans for a better world; but the anger in me had to take action. So I howled as loudly as a tomcat with his tail in a beartrap, and with as much futility. I blamed the Establishment and the fuzz for all man-kind's many woes. But all this was before I became a citizen of the *kingdom*. Before I discovered the great Word that opens the gate to freedom.''

When you asked Spinoza a question you just had to wait for the answer, if you had the patience. I said, ''I do not question your status as a law-abiding citizen. But what bugs me is, why are you in jail? Me, I clobbered a powerful citizen. But a man of peace such as yourself—''

''This happening, truthfully, gives me no small embarrassment, chum. Once upon a time they tossed Christians to lions. They have been clapping them in hoosegows ever since Titus took Jerusalem. Hence, my being in the lock-up is more than a little humiliation.''

''Do you plan on telling me *why* you are here?'' I growled.

''Let patience have her perfect work, comrade. Like it's a weird story. Attend me: what was I doing but watching some dissenters tear down a few flags and burn some stuff—well, maybe not precisely *watching* them—''

''Don't tell me you were caught with a Molotov cocktail in your hand!''

Spinoza raised his hand as if in benediction. ''Indubitably, *no*. What I was attempting to do was dissent with the dissenters! Like I was endeavoring to explain to them the value and the virtue of non-violence, insisting that the great Galilean would never have spit on a decal or fire-bombed even a doghouse. What happened is, when the fuzz came forth and netted a batch of these destroyers I was caught in the selfsame net!''

For the first time in many days I actually laughed aloud. ''Of all the kooky things!''

''Like irony stacked on irony!'' cried Spinoza. ''But would you care to dwell on man's sense of justice? Consider,

75

then, my particular case. I, trying to keep the things from being burned down am ensconced in the same hoosegow with those who burned the things!''

"It's a crazy world," I agreed.

"However, it's like I'll be removed from these undesirable premises immediately—unless, of course, the fuzz are overly deterred in discovering their error."

"Anyhow, we can have a visit. So nice to see you!"

"Forgive my inquisitiveness, friend. But did your lovely frau come to see you?"

"Why?" I demanded quickly.

He waved his hand. "Like I'm aware that she tried to see you, and you were anything but kind to her."

"What are you doing—keeping a diary on what happens between Sally and me?"

"Far be it from me—"

"Look. I walked out on her. I went from the top to the bottom. I wind up in jail. The woman comes to see me. Put yourself in my place. I just couldn't face her. A man has his pride—"

"Like what an oldie!" cried Spin. "A man has his pride! Pride over *what,* baby? Mankind goes about acting like an ape—far worse than a first-class ape! Like he smashes his world up, soaks it in human blood, acts like the devil in general; then when he is slapped flat on his face by his own stupid behavior, he sticks up his head from the gutter and howls,'A man has his pride, you know!' "

"Oh, turn blue!" I said.

"Like a diagnosis is never pleasant, man. But what good is a remedy without a proper diagnosis?"

"Why didn't you stay out of my jail? Did you get stuck in here just to preach sermons to me?"

Spinoza chuckled. "Far be it from me, baby, to take a stand behind the sacred desk—or to appear as a homilist before a captive congregation of one. Like it's trouble enough trying to make believers without being handicapped by being a man of the cloth!''

Silence fell then, except for the jail-noises that floated about the place. Spinoza filled in the silence by beginning to sing in a low voice. ''Rock of Ages, cleft for me—''

After a while I asked, ''About my wife. How are you and she getting along?''

Spinoza both grinned and shrugged. ''Were I to use the word 'cozy' it would be the wrong word. Like you yourself have said, we are both believers. That's how we are getting along—like believers!''

Could be both of you are crazy! I said silently. Aloud, I said, ''Sorry I lost my cool. Nice you could drop by —even under these circumstances.''

''Like it says in the great Book, believers should visit those who are in prison. But quite possibly I shall find myself unrewarded for this visit, seeing I was *forced* to make it!''

Later that night they came and took Spinoza out of the cell, explaining that they were sorry for their mistake. It seemed a couple of dissenters with whom Spinoza argued in favor of non-violence had spoken up for him.

Leaving, Spinoza waved at me through the bars and said, ''Right on with love, baby! Like the great Apostle said, love never quits!''

CHAPTER **13**

WHEN SPINOZA WAS GONE I lay on my hard bunk, sleepless.

What is there about this character that takes hold of you? my mind asked. Obviously, he is a weirdo. But a weirdo that you can't shrug off.

Finally, half-asleep and half-awake, a thought lodged in my mind that brought me fully awake again. That man has some strange power in him! He seems to dare to lift off any masks, to speak truthfully and bluntly, even when he hurts you—yet he, somehow, makes you feel you *need* him! He seems to leave a large empty place when he moves out of your presence!

When I dropped into sleep at last I moved into a dream. The dream was a foggy affair—something about a world wracked in agony and crying for help. But through it all beat the words Spinoza had left me when they took him from his cell.

Right on with love, baby.

The following morning I sat staring at the bars before me. Five months yet to go! One hundred and fifty days. Thirty-six hundred hours. Two hundred and sixteen thousand minutes.

My eyelids came down like curtains over my eyes. Breath whistled softly into my lungs. The back-wash of jail-jargon nagged the edges of my mind while it computerized the time remaining in my sentence.

Time is a funny thing. Either you have too much of it or too little.

"Hey, buddy!" The inmate in the cell next to me said. "Wanna see the papers?"

Accepting the proffered newspaper I sat down to read it. People uptight about the President sending troops into Cambodia. Israel keeping up a constant attack against her ring of enemies. A vast earthquake in Peru. Floods in Rumania. Planes being hijacked.

So the world was carrying on outside my little fenced-in domain.

Seeking the editorial page my eyes got glued on an item in the second section of the paper. Sally's face looked at me from the page. Sally, an accompanying piece said, had a new job. She was working at the Rosewood Children's Home. According to the write-up the children were crazy about her.

Naturally she would have had to take a job. It had been a long time since I had sent her any money. My proud boast that I would see to it that she was taken care of financially had been an empty pledge. When I had made the pledge, of course, money had been a minor item. I had been about to become vice-president of Acme Distributors! A groan squirmed out of me.

One thing made me feel better. Sally would be working with children. Maybe that would make her forget the jailbird who had once traded her for the promise of a high place in Babylon!

Her face smiled at me from the newspaper. Suddenly I crumpled up the newspaper and hurled it on the floor.

"A fouled-up world, buddy, right?" said the man who had given me the paper.

"What difference as long as we're in *here?*" I snapped.

"Yeh, I guess what they do out there don't have much to do with what happens to us here."

My fists balled up tightly. But it *did* matter what they were doing out there! What *some* of them were doing, anyhow. What Sally was doing, for instance.

I put my hands up to my face. *I'm sorry I'm such a stumblebum, Sally.*

CHAPTER **14**

THE CLOCK TICKED OFF the 216,000 minutes.

The streets were under my feet again. The September sun was warm on my face.

My look ran around me; and it was as if it were marking a dead-end street whichever way I looked. The few dollars which the company I had been working for sent me when I was jailed lay lightly in my pocket. It was useless to return to them and ask about a job. The session behind the bars had taken care of that.

Neon-lights gleamed across the street. Andy's Tavern, the lights said. Entering the place I grabbed a bar-stool; and it came to me forcefully that I hadn't had a drink in six months. And I had scarcely noticed the absence of booze!

I looked confidentially at the image in the glass beyond the bar and said silently, *You're not an alcoholic, Gann. You know that?*

"Shot," I told the bartender. "Water back."

I lifted the glass. The stuff glowed in it, amber-colored. It went down in a gulp. The fiery little snake ran down inside me, wriggling deeper and deeper.

No, I wasn't an alcoholic. I was just a lousy drunk!

"Hit me again, Johnny," I said to the barkeep.

"Name's Jerry," he said.

"Mine's Amos," I said cheerfully.

The barkeep chuckled. "Used to hear about a guy with that name. In Sunday school. He was a preacher of some kind. Back in them old Bible days. A real ripsnortin' preacher, I guess, the way they told it." He shrugged. "That's been a long time ago. Since I heard about this Amos, that is."

Which reminded me Sally had once noted that I bore the name of a fiery prophet who denounced the sins of this nation.

This, I told myself, is another time. Another place. The booze hits you hard after you've been off it a while. Another time, another place. This is another Amos. And he's not a fiery prophet.

This is Amos the drunk!

I *was* drunk. Two hours out of jail and I was already stoned.

"Hey, Jerry," I called. "You wanna know something? I just got out of jail."

"That a fact?"

"Lis'en. Been caged up like a maddog. A vicious killer maddog. For six months. I've got to celebrate. I'm looking for some place to get stoned in."

Jerry grinned a little. "Well, old buddy, this isn't the kind of a place where we throw 'em out for feeling a little high. Else we'd be fresh out of patrons. Just stay away from any rough stuff. Don't give me any headaches and I'll get you as drunk as you want, or as your pocketbook will allow."

"S'a deal, old buddy," I chuckled. "A deal is a deal is a deal. Right, old buddy?"

My money, however, held out longer than my capacity for liquor. I knew I was getting too far gone. No use getting knocked out your first night out, old buddy, I warned myself. No fun in that.

In a gathering fog I rose and said to the barkeep, "See you next time I get out of jail. Okay?"

"Get a nice short sentence, buddy."

Negotiating the streets gave me some trouble. I had always prided myself on my ability to handle the souce. This was a perfect time to see how right I had been.

The fog was getting thicker and landmarks becoming more and more indistinguishable. Then out of the gathering gloom appeared a lanky figure which I, even in my condition, recognized.

"Unquestionably," sounded a voice like a Tennessee hound's, "there will be headaches on the morrow, man!"

"How the worl' you track me down like that?" I demanded. "Was positive left no clues whatever. Ironside, so help me. Ol' Ironside—"

"Like I was aware you were being freed from the calaboose today, friend, and since I could get loose from the wheel of labor for a time, I hit for the neighborhood where they let you go. My intuition appears to have been correct. Casing the juice-joints here-abouts who bobs out of one, like a hare from his warren, but yourself?"

"Ver' clever man," I muttered. "Oh, so ver' clever."

"Indubitably," grinned Spinoza. "Like maybe I should be on the staff of Hawaii Five-O."

"Lis'en, fren.' How's about you and me, for ol' time's sake, invading that crummy joint over the way and having a quickie for the road?" I paused and frowned and said, "Hey, what road?"

"You are cognizant that I never belt the grape, my compatriot. And as for you, one more hearty gulp will make you Mr. Nobody from Nowhere. But there comes to me a bright idea. Accompany me to my pad and we will dicuss the pitfalls of boozing it up over a Spinoza Special—a big deep black cup of coffee."

Sometime later we were in Spinoza's pad facing two steaming mugs of the black stuff; but it was a waste as far as I was concerned. I was beyond the reach of anything but sleep. I remember Spinoza drawing a blanket over me as I waded into an alcoholic coma.

Consciousness brought thundering drums in my head and nausea in my stomach. An attempt to sit up wrenched a groan from me. Spinoza loomed over me, holding out a glass of fizzing stuff.

"Like relief is just a swig away, baby. But it's not like I'll guarantee how *much* relief you will discover. But assuredly it won't hurt you as much as all that stuff you've been swigging."

Finally I was propped up in bed, woozy, but en route to some sort of sanity.

"Like wow!" jeered Spinoza. "Like you've been run over by that big beer wagon and the six big horses!"

I groaned. "Like comedy and clowns are no comfort to me at this moment."

"Time was when I loaded up big on the joy-juice," said Spinoza. "And not the juice alone, but pot also. Like, man, I was an authentic gutter-seeker! A self-appointed rebel bent on restructuring all structures whatsoever. Obscene curses upon the Establishment of the Caesars! And on all middle-aged and affluent squares. Like I perused the books by twenty-year-olds who screamed we must trust no one past thirty, and all the time they quoted from half a hundred cats who were far past thirty when they wrote what was being quoted!"

"Yeh," I said.

"But name, if you can, just who it was that I was destroying, if not a cat named Spinoza Jones? But, mark the irony of the thing: all this time I was claiming to be one of the intellectuals of the earth! Try to dig that, baby, and see if it makes sense."

"I'm not exactly in the mood for philosophy," I said.

"What about another shot of that stuff that fizzes?"

When the second fizz-drink was down I was able to move about the room. Wondering how far it was to the nearest tavern, I caught Spinoza eyeing me closely. He said, "Since this pad is not too far removed from the neighborhood where you once lived, you are aware that there is a bar over on Oak Street."

"You," I said, "are a mind-reader. You are also about the nicest Christian I have ever consorted with."

"It could be, comrade, that you once walked out on a far finer Christian!"

"Well, here we go again!" I glowered deeply. "Every time we meet you manage to bring up my wife. Let me ask you a blunt question: are you in love with Sally?"

Spinoza frowned, sighed. "A believer ought not always to become gushy with the truth, maybe. It is sometimes better, maybe, he keeps his big mouth shut! But confronted with a direct question like that you have just posed, maybe I should speak from my heart."

He stopped, then added at once. "Unquestionably, friend, I am in love with your lovely frau!"

Blood must have drained from my face. I took a step in Spinoza's direction. He lifted his hand. "Handle your cool, if you can, chum. You have heard the story in part. This beautiful, incomparable believer whom I love is in love with a donkey-headed cat who scarcely has the gumption to duck under a shed during a hail storm!"

My head throbbed; my feet seemed glued to the floor. And while I struggled to find my tongue for an outburst, Spinoza said, "You have said that I am the nicest Christian you have encountered—"

"I said that, you idiot, before you said what you've just said!"

"Like how many Christians have you ever encountered,

my bar-hugging friend? Have you not always eschewed them that walk by the Word? Doubtless many feel the flame that singed Moses, but far too few take off their shoes! Rather they take off like a jackrabbit from a greyhound!''

"Oh, man! I've had enough of your guff to—''

"Have you reckoned how full the world is of ninny-hammers who cannot bear the Truth? Are they not everywhere, in the marketplace, on the beach, in the woods? You may discover them sitting in judges' seats or teaching in the great academies. Or standing up there in the pulpit also, fearful of speaking the Word of the Lord, making with their sick talk about secularity, peace, and things, fleeing any discussion of a transcendental God who stacked up Creation. They are embarrassed at the mention of that mightiest Event which shall shake history, the Second Coming of Christ. They seek refuge from truth in a big, fat sneer! Has it ever occurred to you how sneers scare people half to death?''

"You," I shouted, "are a lunatic! You ought to be put away somewhere! You shouldn't be allowed to prowl around among sane people!''

"Did you dig, man, what I just said about a big, fat sneer?''

"I'm not sneering! I meant what I said. You're nuts!''

"Consider what stirs up your mad, friend. Because I have told you how mankind flees the truth? Or is it because when you asked me if I love your frau, I told you the truth about that?''

I tried to tie down my ballooning anger; but it got loose. One step forward and I hit Spinoza hard. He stumbled against the wall. When he straightened blood oozed from his nose down to his mouth. He licked the blood from his lips and grinned at me.

"Violence, baby! You really dig it! Consider, if you will, that I am bigger than you and that you have a shaky hangover, while I am in excellent condition. What if I should decide to smatter you over there against that solid wall!"

"Just try it, you maniac!" I howled. "Just try it!"

He wagged his head. "Like you're safe, friend, like a baby in his mama's arms. Have you ever heard what the great Galilean said about turning the other cheek? Have you the urge to clobber me again? Be my guest, comrade!" He stuck out his jaw and waited.

Anger still boiled in me; but instead of hitting him I wheeled to the door. Just as I caught the doorknob in my hand he said, "My pad is yours as long as you wish to use it, friend!"

Turning, I cried, "When I want sermons I'll go to church!"

Spinoza grinned despite his wounded nose. "Like you may never get the kind of sermons at church that make you as angry as the ones you get here, compatriot!"

"Ahhh!" I growled.

"How about a lift? I'll take you wherever you wish to go."

Where did I wish to go? A good question.

Thrusting through the door without replying to Spinoza I walked away from his place. Had he hit me back my anger might have been much less. After walking a while I stopped and said aloud, "What gives with that weird character? How do I keep getting tangled up with him?"

A bar-sign hailed me from afar and I set my course thereto. A man can get to where his sole refuge is a booze-joint.

A couple of whiskey-shots smoothed my hangover considerably. I counted what money I had while I tossed down the shots. The reserve was down to nine dollars. You can't buy too much whiskey with nine dollars. Besides I didn't have a room paid for. Things were getting pretty rough.

"Hit me again, Johnny," I said.

"Name's Harry," he said in a gravelly voice, refilling the glasses.

"You know what, Harry? I just socked a friend of mine."

He examined my face with a look. "You must have put him away. Don't look like he got to you."

"He never hit me back. He never does. He's like that. You never met anybody like Spinoza."

"What kind of a name is that?"

"He named himself."

"Sounds like it."

"You never met anybody like Spinoza," I repeated. "He's in love with my wife."

The barkeeps eyebrows cocked into questionmarks. "That's why you socked him?"

"No, not really. I socked him because of the sermon."

"This guy who's in love with your wife is a *preacher?*"

"Oh, no, he's not a preacher. He just preaches."

Harry shook his head. "You know, friend, you are a little difficult to follow."

I chuckled. "Hit me with a quickie. I have an appointment."

"Not with this friend that you socked who's in love with your wife and preaches?"

The drink burned in my throat. I drew myself to me feet. "No. An appointment with destiny, comrade."

"You a communist, fella?"

"Like a cow loves a T-bone steak!" I chuckled.

The barkeep shook his head as I went to the door.

CHAPTER 15

MY HANGOVER was gently cradled in another binge by the time I had walked a few blocks. A bus stop seat invited me to sit down and ponder things.

It was a fine day. Neither too hot nor too cool. The lovely weather, somehow, made me think of Sally. A vast sadness came over me. I thought of Spinoza Jones and grew angry. I thought of Marvin Bengold and Marilyn Hunter and grew still angrier.

An urge seized me to see Sally again.

Foggy-minded I walked the blocks to the house where Sally and I had lived together. But on reaching it I remembered that Sally wouldn't be home. She would be at the Rosewood Children's Home. I turned away from the drive where I had driven my white convertible so many times. Maybe it was best. How could I meet Sally in my condition, amid old surroundings where we had lived our lives together?

Yet, still foggy-minded, I caught a bus and went to the Rosewood Home. But when I came to the gate I did not go in. Like the play-back of a movie I envisioned the evening when I had asked Sally for a divorce to please Marvin Bengold. Coming back to her like this, over half-drunk, dirty—it would never do.

Turning away from the gate at the home I sensed a terrible sickness gripping me. An unbidden sob tore at my throat.

Later, slumped over a bar, I felt a hand touch my shoulder.

A tall fellow in a crumpled gray suit was beside me, but not on a bar-stool. He was standing.

"Amos Gann?" he asked.

"If anybody cares."

"I care." Then I saw the badge in his hand. He said, "I'll have to ask you to come with me to police headquarters."

"Now, wait a minute. Wait a stupid little minute! The other time I had done something. But what do you want this time?" Then I stared at him. "You don't mean that dizzy Spinoza has preferred charges against me? Why, that two-bit—"

"I know nothing of any Spinoza being associated with this case," said the cop. "You know your rights, I suppose, about having an attorney—"

"Look, I waive any such rights. I have nothing to hide from."

"Last night somebody tried to bomb the Acme Building. In fact they *did* bomb it. Does that ring any bell for you?"

"You must be off your rocker, fellow. I wasn't near the Acme Building last night—"

"Let's go downtown," he said. Then we were in a cop-wagon headed for police headquarters.

More than booze was dazing my mind now. As much as I loathed Bengold the thought had never crossed my mind to bomb the Acme Building. Even drunk I wasn't that stupid! After all, what did they think I was—some rotten criminal? Maybe I was a washed-up drunk, but not a miserable hood!

Still waiving my right to have a lawyer present I allowed them to question me at headquarters. If you ever see a cop who's not full of questions that will be the day. They're worse than the news media.

"You aren't exactly friendly with Mr. Bengold, are you, Mr. Gann?"

"You can say that often, and with emphasis," I snorted.

"You beat him pretty badly once, right?"

"You must have an account of that somewhere in your files. The job cost me six months in your lovely lock-up."

"Where were you last night?"

"Well, part of the time I was in a bar." I named the tavern.

"What time did you leave the tavern?"

I told him, as near as I could recall. "I was pretty swacked. I'm not sure just what time I left. Ask the bartender."

"You were stoned, huh?"

"Enough."

"Drunks sometimes do strange things."

"Like bombing buildings? You're way off. I know nothing whatever about bombs. I couldn't make one if my life was at stake."

"A bomb like that one that damaged the Acme Building is not hard to make."

"It would be impossible for me."

"Where did you go after you left the tavern?"

Here we were. I could tell them I was with Spinoza. He was my alibi. The man who was in love with my wife. The man I had socked yesterday. Was there no way to get away from this character?

Recklessness gripped me for an instant and I almost cried, "Go ahead. Throw the book at me. It's none of your business where I was when I left that tavern!"

But I didn't say it. I thought about those 3,520 hours I'd spent in the pokey and I gave them Spinoza's name and address.

Half and hour later Spinoza arrived at the station. The alibi he gave for me was something of a production.

"Incontestably, comrades, this cat had nothing to do with the havoc wrought in the Acme Building last night. Such a thing is not only incredible, but impossible. At the time you say the bomb exploded Mr. Gann was incapable of blowing up a paper bag! He was utterly incapacitated. Like piflicated, swacked, out like a lantern!"

Evidently after talking with Spinoza for a while the police decided that with him on the witness stand the case for the prosecution would be a real fiasco. So they dismissed me.

Spinoza confronted the brusque arresting officer and said, "Like an apology from you might comfort him somewhat."

"Apology? Look, fellow, I was only doing my job."

"Might part of job possibly be apologizing to a citizen who has been handcuffed and dragged downtown who is quite innocent of any crime? The fact that this citizen is something of a bar-hound and jailbird does not keep him from being a part of the human race—"

"Look—"

"Contemplate this, friend. What if this man were, say, Marvin Bengold, president of Acme Distributors, would you, having taken him into custody, then established his innocence, thrust him forth without an apology?"

"You really run off at the mouth, don't you?" muttered the policeman.

"You may count me at all times on the side of law and order, compatriot. Consider me your friend. But have you thought that haughty attitude on your part might cause some cat to come along some day and refer to you as a pig?"

The cop flushed with anger. "Listen, I've had about all I can take of your gab—"

But behind him a tall man said, "The citizen may have a point, Miller. I think we do owe Mr. Gann an apology. We wouldn't want him to leave thinking of us as pigs, would we now?" He put out a hand toward me. "I'm Lieutenant Mackay. Sorry we caused you an inconvenience, sir."

"Okay," muttered Miller. "Now the man can run along and find a tavern!"

"That, also," said Spinoza, "may be slightly out of the domain of your affairs."

By now the lieutenant was grinning broadly. "Doubtless, Miller, this loyal citizen is correct on a second count."

Miller scowled, grunted, and walked away. Spinoza addressed himself to the lieutenant. "Like the great Apostle says, honor them that are in authority. Which order is made far easier when those in authority are honorable. Such as yourself, compatriot."

As we started for the door I glanced back and the lieutenant was gazing after us, a smile still brightening his face. Arriving at Spinoza's car he said, "The door of my pad is ajar, friend. A thing is nagging my mind that I would like to share with you. Can you spare a little time?"

Time? I could spare a lot of it. But I said, "Look, Spin. Haven't I caused you enough trouble? On top of hitting you on the nose! There's no reason why you should concern yourself this much with me, even if—"

When I hesitated Spinoza grinned. "Even if I *am* in love with your lovely frau?"

What do you do with a character like that?

We drove to his pad. Inside I said, "I'm filthy, Spin. I could do with a bath."

He chuckled. "Have you heard that the great newsman, Ernie Pyle, once said, 'If you go long enough without a bath even the fleas will let you alone'? One should not chance being an outcast from the society of fleas."

The bath helped. A shave also helped.

"If your sense of well-being has kept pace with your appearance, then you have traveled far," said Spinoza.

Digging up a grin I dropped into a chair. "Let's face it. I don't exactly feel like a vice-president!"

"The cat who can laugh at himself is not to be laughed at!" said Spinoza.

CHAPTER **16**

ALL AT ONCE SPINOZA turned on a record player and rock music assaulted my eardrums.

I stared at him. "You go for that sort of thing?"

He shrugged. "Some of it, that part which I do not abhor. Like we have to make choices in such a world as ours. Ever and anon some cast comes up with a pop-thing that has in it better theology than one may hear in many sermons these days. Like that thing: *Who Will Answer?* Or like *Skip-A-Rope*. Like, man, they now have one on the Book of Revelation! Are there not numerous clergymen who will not so much as consider the great Apocalypse? How many pulpits, do you suppose, have become utterly silent regarding this awesome last book in the great Book?"

"I'm not too hep to what comes out of pulpits these days," I said, hoping Spinoza wouldn't get going on theology, and more especially on eschatology! One more sermon, I felt, would about finish me!

"I don't mind rock music," I said.

"What you need, baby, is a great T-bone steak, broiled as it should be broiled, with a dash of Worcestershire sauce, and some fried potatoes. Fried in corn oil. Corn oil is good for you. Are you aware of that?"

The steak was all Spinoza promised. It gave me strength, even lifted my spirit somewhat. The need for a drink seemed negligible after the meal I had eaten.

Dinner finished, Spinoza said, "Should you have a mind to it, the boobtube awaits us. Color, no less. For myself, outside the news and a few other shows, scarcely do I squander time on the mighty medium."

The first thing to attack me when I switched on the TV was a wild man selling automobiles. Then came an item about what harm cigarettes could do to you, and a few moments later a cigarette commercial. Then a man was making bad jokes, each joke followed by a wave of canned laughter.

"Maybe," I told Spinoza, "we'd better stick to rock."

"A better idea comes to me, friend. I did not invite you here specifically to hear rock music. Like I told you, a thing nags my mind: the news of a strange fortune."

"Fortune?"

Spinoza went to a drawer and came out with some legal-looking documents. "Maybe I have told you that my mama died when I was a baby. My papa was of the Establishment, and he made it big. In a way we were close, but in another we were light years apart. Unquestionably I loved him, and I have reason to think he loved me also. But love has an odd way, betimes, of jumping out of orbit. Like polarization between me and my papa finally caused me to cut out."

He paused, said, "My papa died a few years ago, and his estate, naturally, was grabbed at from sundry sides. But finally comes this strange happening: quite a bundle of his fortune falls in my lap!"

"Hmmm," I said. "Well, congratulations."

"Money?" cried Spinoza. "Ignorant men have said it is the root of all evil. Which is the gabble of fools. Does not the great Book inform us that the *love* of money is the evil thing? The love of its power—think on that! Consider a charming woman from America and her mate from overseas spending twenty million dollars on a honeymoon! How many revolutions do you think a thing like that could trigger in the minds of cats who creep about the earth never free from want? Mark the warning in the great Book—*Go to now, you rich men, weep and howl for the miseries that shall come upon you!* Money—it's an awesome thing, baby!"

"Money may be awesome," I muttered, "but things can get pretty awful without it!"

Spinoza agreed with a head-motion. "Like money can be wonderful, chum! Consider what things you can do with it. You can put food in the mouth of a poor little big-bellied starving baby! Contemplate that, friend! You can warm them who turn blue from cold. Like, man, you can work the work of God with it!"

Spinoza sprang up from his chair and began tramping about the room. *"Have you ever read in the great Book: Money answereth all things?* Like money is power, and power is the test of the human spirit. Why, do you think, the great Galilean kept talking about the stuff? Almost one might discover a dollar-sign tucked away in every parable He uttered!

"Baby, it's like I have in my hands a fortune left by a giant of the Establishment—yet I tremble when I think what gales can break upon the Establishment because the Establishment has forgotten what to do with money!"

Spinoza stood a moment wagging his head. Then he said, "But let us return to an idea that takes hold of me. I have in my hands enough Mammon to build a small kingdom. And I am convinced I can make much more money than I now have. The Lord has made me a mechanic—and the Lord's mechanics are not to be scoffed at! So, I shall build machines. I will build many fine machines. Like I will join the technocratic rat-race that may be threatening mankind with doom, according to the ecologists! You are reading me?"

"Like through a horse blanket!" I said.

"Have you any passion for machines? Well, no matter. I plan to put you in charge of sales, anyhow!"

"Now, wait a minute. Do you feel okay? You are talking to a man who was kicked out of ordinary sales work because he lapped up the booze! You're talking to a jailbird. And you are talking of some kind of important business, some enterprise. Look—they don't stick misfits in high places!"

Spinoza fairly leered at me. "Did you not get rather high with Acme Distributors?"

"That was then. Things have changed. *I* have changed. Don't you realize that? I'm not the same man who was close to the top at Acme's. Maybe you should take a closer look at me before you start throwing some big job at me!"

"Faces!" roared Spinoza.

"Faces?"

"Why do we forever look at faces and think we have all the lowdown on a cat? Faces change from the time we come squalling into this world until we cut out for the cemetery. But this thing in us which we call life—whatever it is—that's something otherwise. Attend me, friend. The gutter is never for anyone except those who really *want* it. Like do *you* want it, baby?

While I reached for something to say Spinoza was off and running again. "Like the great Apostle said, forget those things that are behind you. Accompany me, friend, into my enterprise and I will render you an avowal: in that corner of the Establishment where I speak every cat will have his chance to do his thing—and only God will play God!"

I grabbed a long breath. "You're too much for me, Spin. I'm glad you have money; I think you deserve it more than most men. I hope you'll have success with your enterprise. It could well be the Establishment needs a million guys like you! But regarding *me*—I haven't the foggiest idea what I'm going to do."

"Indubitably. Allow yourself time to cogitate."

"Listen, Spin." I spread out my hands. "Remember who I am? A drunk. A bum who has been kicked out of commonplace jobs. You talk about giving me a responsible place in an important business?"

"Comrade, while I am perusing the great Book I get the joyous feeling that it matters not so much what a cat is as what he may become!"

"Wait. Say I took you up on your proposition. Where is any assurance I won't crack up and let you down? I've done it before. Again and again. Shall I be honest? Do you know where I'd like to be this minute?"

"My initial guess, friend, is hanging on to a barstool somewhere, drowning whatever manhood you still have left!"

"Okay," I snapped. "Well, *okay!*"

Spinoza fixed me with a penetrating look. He flipped back a strand of blond hair that had dropped over one ear. "Is it like definitely you are going to howl for those mountains?"

"Mountains?"

"To fall on you, baby, and get you out of the sight of that big Throne! Is it imperative that you be part of this hollow-headed and hollow-hearted world that lives and moves in this stupid time? Shall the prophet cry aloud and spare not and show Israel her sins in vain? How is it that you cannot hear the trumpet warning you to flee the wrath to come? Why have the fears of the damned been tranquilized?"

"Oh, for the love of Pete—!" I wailed.

"Like I'm asking you to come away from that void, man! Who else but you can make the turn? Have you never heard what the great Isaiah said? *Watchman, what of the night?* How many do you suppose have had the morning in their grasp, but let it go, and were swallowed up in the night?"

His deluge of words brought back an old anger, but at the

same time they left me with a definite fear. This was a voice foreign to most of that race known as Americans. It was the voice of Judgment.

The voice hammered at me some more. "It is an awesome time for a witness when he must push his friend to the edge of the void—it is an awesome risk that the witness must take, however! It is the way of the great Book, and the great Galilean; one must come to the end before he can find the beginning. There is a death-march to life, friend. There is no resurrection this side of Calvary!"

All the best sense in me that the booze had not yet drowned took sides with the weird, unordained proclaimer of the Word. Somewhere the downhill runner must stop and turn and start back up the steep. Or, in Spinoza's words, comes the void.

"What a preacher is wasted in you!" I said.

"Far be it from me to take the sacred desk—"

"I know. I know. Will you answer me a question outright?"

"Equivocation is not my thing."

"Tell me *why* you labor so hard to get me out of the gutter? Why do you hang on? Why don't you let me go? What's in it for you?"

Spinoza rubbed his chin meditatively. "For one thing, friend, I'm in love with your lovely frau!"

"Oh, for heaven's sake! How many times do I have to hear that? You make no sense whatever. If you're in love with my wife, why don't you let me go on down the drain? That would give you a chance to have her!"

"Oh, slow of heart to understand!" wailed Spinoza. "What do you want for that one you love except happiness? The woman I love is in love with *you,* you ox-headed barfly! Far be it from me to philosophize *why* she is in love with you! But you are the one who can make her heart make like the wing-dance of a butterfly!''

"Will you listen a minute—''

"Like who is it that should be listening? Inform me how I can give you to that lovely woman when you are parked on a jail bunk or perched on a barstool? When you haven't got a pad to come home to or a hunk of bread in the bank? Am I coming through to you, man?''

An odd shaking began inside me. This was out of the world; it was weird. It was some unreal dream taking up time on TV. Yet it wasn't a dream. Spinoza Jones wasn't just saying words. He was talking out of some inner urge and agony. Out of some heartbreak.

The force of realizing this practically brought tears to my eyes.

But Spinoza wasn't finished yet. There was more in him. It came out in a torrent. "The reason I have given for my concern over you is the minor one. Have you ears to hear the major one? Possibly you may have read in a big news magazine lately an item that said like this: those who still believe God can give a person eternal life live surrounded by an alien culture. And it happens like I'm one of those who so believe. It happens Caesar does not own my soul! I am a citizen of Otherworld. My allegiance is to the Kingdom.

"Like I look down the dead-end streets in this world. Where is the answer to man's needs? I do not find them in Caesar's domain, nor would I expect to, in a million years! This dog-gobble-dog setup races toward a nihilistic future. Did not the great Albert Schweitzer say, 'This civilization is doomed'?

"There are those of us who cannot join the cosmic rat-race. Like we are overwhelmed by another Drummer! Like we have an appointment with destiny, baby! Like we are on our way to meet a King!''

Spinoza paused a moment; then he said, "Forgive me my

many words, friend; but it appeared to me that I must explain my position in this world-jungle so I might say to you in the interim that before I meet this King I have vast responsibilities here and now. And one of these responsibilities is none other than *yourself!*''

''Wait—have I ever asked you to look after me?''

''To be sure, no. It is *God* who put you on my hands. And should you trek off to the wastelands, then I shall have in a measure failed also. I *am* my neighbor's keeper, comrade! You are reading me?''

Before I could muster a yes or no Spinoza went on. ''Imagine not, friend, that it is *you* only whom I am concerned about. Shall I inform you that when I get my business going I shall go out in the dead-end streets and compel them to come in? How many barflies and jailbirds do you suppose there are that need to stand up and walk like men?''

''You must be off your rocker, Spin! You mean you'll drag in riff-raff and misfits to handle your business? How long do you think it will last?''

''Like it's not my business, man, but the Almighty's! Contemplate how much backing one might get from Cosmic Center when he is engaged in doing business for the Lord!''

''Your reference to the riff-raff and the misfits—not all men who appear as riff-raff are in reality riff-raff; and I, the good Lord helping me, am not altogether without discernment! And have you thought I want these men interested only in what we call progress, success, or democracy? It is in my mind to betray them into the hands of Him who took the hoodlum's beam to that Hill!

''Let all the misguided theologians in this misguided world look askance at that big New Testament word: but it's like I want to get these cats *saved,* baby!''

CHAPTER 17

SLEEP KEPT ITS DISTANCE from me far into the night. Lying in Spinoza's pad, I was locked in a war with my own spirit. The struggle grew so intense that I even forgot that I needed a drink!

Two voices clamored for a hearing in my consciousness. One urged me to leap out of bed and head for the house where Sally lived. But the other voice argued that this would be madness, that something would have to happen to me personally before I could go to her. Something *big* would have to happen. Something so private that is was rather terrifying to think of it.

When sleep finally came, disturbing dreams came with it. What all the dreams were about I cannot recall; but in one of them Spinoza Jones's voice was booming out at intervals: *"There is a death-march to life, baby!"*

Morning brought with it the awareness that the day was Sunday. In Spinoza's kitchen was the smell of bacon and eggs and coffee.

As I came into the kitchen Spinoza waved a spatula at me and almost shouted: "This is the day that the Lord has made; let us be glad and rejoice in it!"

I answered him with a scowl and a grunt.

"Following a repast I am bound for the house of the Lord," Spinoza announced.

"That figures," I muttered.

"Like it says in the Book: *not forsaking the assembling of yourselves together, as the manner of some is . . . and so much the more as you see that Day approaching.*"

"What day is that?" I asked, realizing too late what could be triggered by the question.

"Like the Day of the Lord, man, what else? Unquestionably that Day is not as far off as many may think—when the Visitor from outer space who touched down at a tavern-keeper's cowbarn will touch down again on our troubled earth."

"You really believe that will happen, don't you?"

"Convince me I should disbelieve it! Did He not promise to do it? Is He not the cosmic Gentleman?"

"That coffee smells good," I said.

Spinoza chuckled. "Eschatology before breakfast may not be too wise a thing." He poured me a cup of coffee. "I trust you like your eggs over easy."

As we ate Spinoza murmured, "Apparently we shall have a fine day for worshiping the Creator."

"You'll probably—" I said, hesitated, then said, "You'll probably see Sally there."

"Undoubtedly the lovely lady will be up there singing in the choir. Might I also add that both her face and her voice do not in any way detract from the appearance and efficiency of the choir?"

I shrugged and took a long pull at my coffee-mug. Spinoza said, "While you slept this morning early I took the liberty of attending somewhat to your raiment. Seeing you wear a drip-dry shirt I attended to it. The thought in my mind was that you might be disposed to attend church with me, and I knew you wouldn't want to wear a dirty shirt. I also pressed your suit. It could be you noticed that when you put on your pants."

My hand swung up. "That's out! That church deal, I mean. I'll hang around here until you get back. But thanks for taking care of the clothes. Remind me to give you a tip!"

But as the time approached for Spinoza to depart for church an inward nagging overcame me.

"It's been a long time since I held down a pew," I said.

"Like too long maybe," said Spinoza.

It was a fine day for going to church—or for going anywhere for that matter. September had done a nice job on the world. Things looked bright enough even to fool Ralph Nader into thinking everything was all right.

But nearing the church door my feet began to be like two big rocks. I almost turned back and let Spinoza go in alone. But he put a mocking grin on me that angered me enough to thrust on through the door.

We found a seat close to the rear. I was glad that a big fellow in front of me practically hid me from the rostrum. The choir was beginning to sing. My look caught on Sally, standing there wearing her white-collared dark robe. She didn't see me, and I was grateful.

My mind tried to say something to her across the distance: funny, I never noticed before how beautiful you look in a choir robe!

The hymn was about the cross. The music washed down on me like surf rolling in from a sea. But the music did not lift me. It hurt me. It threatened to drive me back into the streets in quest of a tavern!

But it was Sunday. The taverns wouldn't be open. Anyhow, unseen chains bound me to my seat, a captive, hammered by a wave of relentless music about a cross.

Out of the voices of the group I picked up Sally's; and it was sweet. Something inside me seemed about to give way.

Tears invaded my eyes. I hated myself for them, but had not power to stop them. They were tiny gobs of fire, wounding my eyes. My heart staggered under a burden too great for a drunk to bear!

Sally's singing was like a woman praying. She was sending words and music out to God. How would it be if I should rush up there and grab her in my arms and cry, "Honey, I am a big idiot!"? But the distance up there to where she was, of course, was immeasurable. I'd never get that far on the power I had.

We were still in two different worlds.

The choir finished its hymn. Dr. Blake arose and began to speak, beginning with something from the Bible. *Come unto me all you that labor and are heavy laden, and I will give you rest.*

Rest! There's a word to think about.

I was tired. I was tired and sick. Sick of all the goings-on in a sick world. A world that had more head than heart—and sometimes you wondered if it even had a *head*. Sick of the mindless drive for *things,* for power, the deadly combat over position and money.

Most of all, sick from trying to find a hiding place in a bottle.

"Man's homesick spirit travels far," said Dr. Blake, "and comes on ghost-towns that mock his quest. No man will ever be home until finally he is home with God."

Beside me, in a barely audible whisper, Spinoza said, "Amen, man!"

Just then Sally's eyes found me in the congregation. Her face paled a little; she tried to smile, and I tried to smile, too. But neither came off too well. Then she put her head down I knew she was praying.

I had never thought before that it could be a lovely thing to see a woman praying!

Suddenly the minister was pronouncing the benediction. Something like a small panic seized me. I eased out of the pew and fled for the door.

Spinoza grabbed my arm. "Like she will want to see you, man."

But it was like I wasn't about to let her catch up with me. People got in my way as I moved on. I wheeled toward Spinoza and said, "Talk to her! I'll see you at your place."

Crashing through a group of people and past the minister at the door, I found the street and walked hard until I came to a bus stop. I alighted from the bus a few blocks from Spinoza's pad and walked toward it.

My eyes ran up and down the street trying to locate a tavern. Finding one I hurried toward it, then remembered it was Sunday. But I stood for a time gazing at the unlighted sign.

Booze! I said in silence. *What a joke! Here I am offered a top position when I'm wallowing at the bottom of the ditch—and I'm looking for a refuge from my good fortune in a stinking juice-joint!*

Something Spinoza had once said to me came back to my mind. "It's not like man is crazy; it's like he's not in his right mind."

I began walking toward Spinoza's pad.

When Spinoza arrived he chided me for running out on Sally. "Despite your fear of humiliation, friend, the lovely woman was not by any means slighty distraught!"

"I couldn't help it," I gritted. "Whether you realize it or not."

"My understanding of things is not altogether defective. How shall the mighty who have fallen stand in the presence of the queen—especially the queen whom he has betrayed!"

"What bugs me is: how long will I put up with your insults?"

"Must you jettison your cool, comrade? Why must the truth always be so offensive? How would *you* say it?"

"You are like some weird lawyer! He asks the witness a dirty question, expecting an objection from the opposition which the judge will support, then he withdraws the question! It's all nice and legal and everyone is happy—but the dirty question is still hanging there in everyone's mind!"

"Far be it from me to make like an attorney, friend. Is there something hanging there in your mind?"

"Brother!" I exploded. *"B-r-o-t-h-e-r!"*

Spinoza laughed lightly. After a brief silence he said, "Circumstantially, it becomes my duty to call on a certain cat, to query him about accepting a place in my coming setup. Like he's a top cat with machines, but our insensitive culture has given him some tough breaks. Of a truth his is something of a mean cat, a dissenter spelled with a capital D, a fire-eater out of the ghetto who got beat up often by his mama and papa and the big kids in the neighborhood, and later clobbered somewhat by the fuzz. Nonetheless, this cat has managed to get a few miles out of his boyhood jungle and his is laboring hard to make himself an authentic member of the homo sapiens tribe. Not that he is out of the stinkweeds yet, but he's working at it.

"Why do I brief you in this manner regarding this cat? Like if he starts throwing the rebel-yak like flak—about how you've got to blow the world up to save it—you'll understand."

"I must have missed something. I don't even know the guy."

"Like you'll meet him when we visit him this afternoon."

"When *we* visit him?"

"You are invited to accompany me."

"Aw, look—"

"Consider this man's frau, friend. She is something other

than this cat she married. It's the lady that I am bent on seeing.''

"Oh. His *wife,* huh?"

"Irrefragably. This cat's frau is a *believer,* and like she's been praying for this gifted husband of hers, this cat who knows machines but is addle-headed regarding ideology. This admirable woman has been hit by a mean illness, and my thought is to comfort her somewhat by a visit. I am coming through to you?''

"Like clear," I grumbled. "But I can't see why you want me to go with you."

I went with him.

As Spinoza had said this man, whose name turned out to be Jeff Bailey, lived not too far from the slums on the West Side. Inside his house I discovered immediately that Jeff Bailey was very big and very black.

Bailey eyed me coldly when we shook hands after Spinoza's introduction. Nor was his handshake warm. He had a rugged-looking face, a face set against an alien world. His sick wife was bright and friendly and warm in her greeting. In fact she glowed in spite of her illness.

During the time we were there I felt uncomfortable each time I caught Bailey looking at me. I thought of a great black cat eyeing those who had put him in a cage.

When Spinoza and I were en route for his pad I said, "That guy acted like I was an unwanted mother-in-law who had moved in permanently."

"Like you're *white,* baby."

"White? What do you mean, white? Nobody is likely to take *you* for a Nigerian."

"Like he sees white when he sees you, but he sees past my skin when he sees me, inasmuch as he knows me and *believes* in me. Like he forgets I'm white. Not that he believes like I believe when it comes to religion, seeing he is an unbeliever, but he believes in *me.* You dig that?"

"Oh, sure. But come the revolution he grabs up a gun along with some fellow revolutionaries, and he'll probably knock you off as quickly as he would me!"

Spinoza wagged his head. "We are not in agreement at that point. But should it turn out you are right, even so he shall have knocked off someone who really cared for him. Have you heard how it was with the great Galilean? Did He stand forth and say, 'Look, everybody, if you prove that you love Me I will go out and die for you on that Hill'? When does love ever ask any favors of anyone, baby?"

Glancing out the car window I said, "Maybe we ought to discuss that new business you're going to set up. I'd like to know more about what you really have in mind for me."

"Six days there are, man, in a week to take care of business. Twenty-six days a month. Three hundred and twelve days a year. Is it imperative that we discuss business on the Lord's day?"

CHAPTER 18

IN THE SPACE of a few days several things happened in Steel City.

For one thing the police located the radicals who bombed the Acme Building. Evidently there had been neither a real reason nor a thought-out plan for the bombing. It was a tall symbol of the Establishment; so it was assaulted.

But the arrest of the militants only triggered loud noises from other militants. One bitter riot resulted in the burning of two more buildings in the city.

"You know what I think?" I said to Spinoza.

"Like I'm tuned in, friend."

"That buddy of yours, that Jeff Bailey; he's probably mixed up in these goings-on. I have the feeling he's a communist."

Spinoza shrugged expansively. "That cat is no communist, comrade. Like he's a little wild, maybe. Too far to the left, but no communist. Like he's a beat-down, long-frustrated, muddled-up American wearing a black skin. Like hate is churning his brains up; but the chances are slight that he ever read *Das Kapital*, or read any speeches by Nick Lenin. How many millions of other cats do you suppose there are in this land of the free and the home of the brave, mixed-up, black, white, brown, who all might be beautiful, but life, minus the Spirit of life, turns them ugly!"

Spinoza secured a site for his new machine plant. The contractors were busy laying the foundation for the buildings. It was to be a large setup; and Spinoza was eager to see it finished and ready for business.

A vast change had come over me. I was actually looking forward to working with Spinoza in his enterprise. Lately I had passed the tavern-bars as if they were garbage cans, even though a couple of times I felt the fierce urge to grab a few quickies. My ability to walk away from the bottle was growing amazingly. I began to sense a new aliveness in me. And a new hope.

Sunday came again. But I did not go with Spinoza to Sally's church. I felt I would not be able to bear seeing her in the choir. I stayed at home and turned on TV.

What did I fish out of the air but a religious service! A fellow was speaking who was a sort of small-sized Billy Graham.

Something he said stuck in my mind. "Consider this question: how shall a man contact God? The answer is that however a man *ever* contacted God, that is how he does it now. There is no gadgetry to help us at this point. You never saw God on television or heard Him on radio. Man can invent no machine which will help usher him into God's presence. Technocracy may work wonders; but it fails at the entrance of the eternal world.

"The one way to contact the Almighty remains forever. We are held to this one point: prayer. We must approach God as man did millennia ago: nor may our approach be varied. He requires of modern man what He required of ancient man: sincerity, humility, repentance, surrender to his sovereignty. He cannot be wheedled for His stance!"

When I had clicked off the television I sat and thought about Sally praying for me in the choir last Sunday at church. How many prayers had she prayed for me?

Would her prayers be answered?

When Spinoza came in he said, "Like you missed the Word from a groovy prophet!"

"I heard it from a fairly groovy prophet on TV."

"Adventitiously, friend, I had words with your engaging frau. And what does she desire but to come here to my pad and see you? I, however, dissuaded her."

"Why?"

"My contention was like this. Why should she be running after a bubbleheaded cat that knows where she lives and who is the one who should be running after her?"

"There are times when I feel like an utter idiot sticking around you! Can nothing keep your nose out of my affairs?"

"Like when do I mess with your affairs, man? My advice was not to you, but to the lovely woman with the sad heart!"

I ripped off a few cuss words that jarred Spinoza visibly. Nor did I apologize. A voice in me seemed to cry: you can't keep on with this impossible character! Even if he does offer you a good job and a chance to get back on your feet. He'll drive you kooky, given time!

Striding to the door I said, "I'm going for a walk. If I never come back you will know that at last I have found you completely insufferable!"

Behind me, as I grabbed the doorknob, Spinoza said, "It eludes me the name of the philosopher who said, 'Your friend is the one who knows you, knows all about you, and loves you just the same'!"

I took the walk and walked for a long time.

I came back.

Two nights later Spinoza Jones lay in the hospital with a knife-gash in him that was deep enough to kill a tiger.

CHAPTER **19**

AT ST. MARY'S HOSPITAL they wouldn't let me see Spinoza. They informed me he was in a very serious condition. When I went to the police station they were polite—and not very talkative.

Listening to the news on local TV, and reading the *Chronicle,* gradually I got the story fairly well pieced together.

Spinoza had gone to the neighborhood where Jeff Bailey lived. Evidently he had gone to discuss business with Bailey. But while he was there something of a riot broke out a few blocks distant; and both Spinoza and Bailey went to see what was happening.

En route to the trouble-spot Bailey said to Spinoza: ''The cat that's triggering this ruckus is a friend of mine. He's a real mean cat, and he's maybe switchblade happy, especially if he's high. What I've got to do is try and get to him and see if I can stop him before he puts somebody away permanently.''

The trouble-maker's name was Hadley. By the time Spinoza and Bailey reached him another man was stretched out at Hadley's feet on the sidewalk with blood turning the sidewalk red. Bill Hadley was straddling the fallen man with a blood-smeared knife clenched in his hand.

Bailey advanced quickly to where Hadley stood. He said, ''You hold it, Bill. You hear me? You want to get your fool self knocked off?''

"You lay back, Jeff," Hadley warned. "You listen to me. This cat here on this sidewalk is a real Judas. So you keep out of it. This is my rumble, baby! I ain't finished with this cat yet, 'cause he ain't dead yet! I'm gonna cut him some more, man, until he won't ever go singing to the fuzz again!"

"You get rid of that knife, you fool!" yelled Bailey. "I'm your friend, remember? You gimme that blade, man!"

Hadley moved stiff-legged away from his fallen victim toward Bailey. The knife gleamed in his grip. "You want to keep breathing, Jeff, you keep a-coming!"

Spinoza sprang past Jeff and faced Hadley. "Like it's no good, friend. Like you don't cut up your old buddy, Jeff. Right?"

Hadley's wild look shot past Spinoza to Bailey. "You throwing Whitey at me now, Jeff? You really lay it on me, don't you, baby? You want me to take him out before I take this Judas out?"

He moved swiftly toward Spinoza. Bailey yelled, "You acid-headed idiot! You kooked-up—"

"Like this!" cried Hadley.

The steel sank to the shaft in Spinoza's body.

The police report said Hadley had been tripping on LSD. They arrived in time to save Bailey and the man on the sidewalk whom Hadley had knifed. But it seemed they had not arrived in time to save Spinoza—according to the doctor's report.

Finally, at Spinoza's request, I was allowed to see Spinoza for a few minutes.

He managed a faint grin.

"Like who knows what fortune, or misfortune, awaits you at any bend of the road, man—"

"Spin!" I dropped down on my knees by the bed. "I'm sorry. I'm more sorry than I ever can say—"

Spinoza fought his way out of a darkness that I sensed was closing in on him.

"What cat knows where he has to take this trip?"

Catching his arm I said, "You'll be okay, Spin. You'll be out in a few days."

He tried to make a negative gesture with his head on the pillow. "Unquestionably you will turn out a false prophet, comrade! But will you not allow it to get you too uptight? Attend a secret: like I have plans to live forever!"

"You'll snap out of it—" Then I said something I had never dreamed I would say. "God will see you through, right?"

Spinoza tried hard to grin. But he didn't do too well with it. A spasm of pain cut off the grin. "Indubitably, friend. But not in the manner you mean!"

Grief clamped hot fingers around my throat. Spinoza said huskily, "Like they don't talk about death in these times. But the great Book talks about it. Tell me, chum, would you think death would be the end of a cat like me?"

You idiot! I cried in silence. *Talking your wild talk at a time like this.* Aloud I said, "I doubt it, Spin. I doubt it very much." Tears tried to rush past my guard. Then I said something I had not intended saying: "Men like you probably never die!"

At that Spinoza mustered up a ragged grin. "Join me, friend, in the big Setup! Has not the great Galilean said, *He that believes in me, though he were dead, yet shall he live; and whosoever lives and believes in me shall never die?*"

A sob assaulted by throat. I managed to say, "Okay, friend—okay."

"Like one thing bugs me, comrade," The voice that was once like a booming hound's was weakening fast "Like I never did get you in condition spiritually so you could put in a few prayers for me at a time like this—"

He closed his eyes and seemed drifting away. Then he rallied and put one last look on me. His voice was very low but each word sank into my heart.

"Right on with love, baby! Great Apostle said—love—never—quits—"

I let the tears loose then. And even in this age when men pride themselves on hiding their emotions, I would have felt like some sort of a traitor if I hadn't wept.

"It never quits—baby!" I said.

CHAPTER 20

SPINOZA JONES CLOSED his eyes and cut out for that World of which he is a citizen—wherever, or whatever, it may be.

An inutterable loneliness caught me in a chest-smashing grip. I rose up from my knees and walked away and left my dead friend with his God.

Walking blindly from the room I banged into a big man. For a moment I failed to recognize him. But he called my name and I saw it was Jeff Bailey. Looking back to that instant I suppose I didn't look altogether *white* to him at the time; for he put a big grip on my arm and said, "How is he?"

Looking at him through tears I said, "He's okay. He's okay, man. But maybe you'd better ask me *where* he is instead of *how!*"

"You mean—he's cut out?"

"Yeh. Cut out. Gone. Wherever he is, men like you and me will never visit him—unless we change our ways regarding what we do with God—and with each other!"

His look held mine hard for a time. I saw his dark eyes fighting the tears. "You reckon what's wrong with religious people—you reckon men like you and me just don't see enough of his kind of believer to impress us big?"

I nodded. "I reckon, friend."

I went out of the hospital into a lonely night and into an empty world.

Spinoza's pad was more empty than the world, and more lonely.

The streets were my refuge again.

The tavern-signs flashed challengingly everywhere. One of them got through to me. Something had to be done about this bottomless desolation inside me.

"Shot," I said to the bartender.

My fingers shook as I raised the small glass of amber-colored stuff to my mouth. The stuff touched my tongue and I put the glass down. Some of the stuff splashed on the bar.

"Something wrong, fellow," asked the barkeep.

"Yeh." I looked at him. "Something's wrong."

"Like what, Mac?"

"Like my mind. Like my life. Like, mostly, my washed-up soul!"

"Look, fellow. Don't start no cryin' jag in here, okay?"

The vernacular of Spinoza Jones was inescapable at that moment. "It's not like I don't need to cry, baby. It's like I'm not in the right place at the right time!"

The bartender's look followed me all the way to the door. I went back to Spinoza's pad and cried.

I cried hard and for quite a while.

I needed Spinoza very much. There comes a time when, if you've been wrong long enough, and you're sick of being wrong, that you need a certain kind of person to show you the right way. Not necessarily a preacher, or a theologian, or even a psychiatrist. He may be a square from nowhere; but he has to have a spiritual mind.

When you don't have that sort of person handy, you have to carry on anyhow, and see what happens. For when this thing finally gets through to you, you're caught in the great rapids until the quiet sea lifts you on its tide.

The words of both Spinoza Jones and Dr. Blake came back to me. *There is a death-march to life.* You never make that march with your mind only. The cynic-devil in you won't let your mind work like that. Reason, disciplined to treason against God's high order, is too much for you.

You reach Him with your heart.

Something happens in that laboratory where motives are made. I could almost have sworn I heard Spinoza saying, "Like you've latched on to the truth. Ride with it, man!"

I rode with it.

I rose from my knees, touched by a Power that had never touched me before. I circled the lonely room a couple of times, then grabbed the phone. I heard it ringing at the other end of the line. My heart hammered.

When Sally's voice came to me I said, "You don't know me. I am a stranger to you—"

"Who is this?" Sally whispered. Then she cried, "Stranger? You're no stranger—"

"Oh, but I am!" I told her. "You never knew me. You knew an idiot who wore my face!—"

"Amos!"

"Listen, Sally. Can I come and see you?"

Silence, then. A silence that cut into me like a switchblade. No spontaneity. She had to have time to think about it! She broke the silence with "All right, Amos."

I winced at the way she said it. Once she would have cried, "Yes! Oh, yes, Amos!"

I shaved carefully, bathed, put on my cleanest shirt. I put on some sweet-smelling lotion I found in Spin's bathroom. When I arrived at Sally's place she was wearing a pale blue dress. Her face was pale, her eyes full of questions.

She said in a small voice: "Hello, Amos."

"Hello, Sally." My voice wasn't much bigger than hers.

I followed her into the living room and saw the picture of Spinoza Jones on the table. Spinoza was grinning, and I could fairly hear him say, "Like you're here, so get on with it, man!"

Sally saw me gazing at the picture and she said, "Why do men like him have to die? It seems so unfair!"

I took in a long breath. "You loved him a lot, didn't you?"

She nodded. Tears glittered far back in her eyes. "How could I help it? He was a real *man,* Amos!" She stopped, then added, "More than that, he was God's man."

"He was in love with you," I muttered. "Very much."

Her head nodded slowly. "I know. But I was a wife. I had a husband!"

Pain hit me inside. "A stupid, drunken husband! Why didn't you get a divorce?"

"Don't think I wasn't tempted! Have you any idea what life meant to me—after you threw me over for a mess of pottage? You traded me off—for *what?* I wept and I prayed—and finally I got to where I quit caring. Then Spin came—and I was at least able to go on living!"

"Sally—"

"A divorce?" She lifted her shoulders and let them down again. "You knew Spin. You know me."

"I know. You are both Christians." I gazed at Spin's picture again. "He was something of a saint, I guess."

"Yes. He never realized it, but he *was* a saint."

"Not the goody-good kind, though."

"The New Testament kind," she said, letting a long breath fill her lungs.

Standing there looking at her it came to me that I had never really quit loving her. Pride had made me sin against her. Then shame had kept me away from her. I was ashamed now. I said, "Sally, I doubt if you'll ever be able to forgive me for what I did to you. A man can't get any lower than I got. But I am sorry. More sorry than words can say." Tears were in my voice. I couldn't keep them out.

"Amos—"

"I won't even blame you if you never forgive me. I'll probably never know what I owe you. Spinoza led me out of the jungle. But who knows how much your prayers helped?"

"—out of the jungle?" she repeated.

"Yes. I am a *believer,* Sally!"

"Oh, Amos!" Then she was in my arms. "How I thank God!"

I held her tight kissing her again and again, tasting her tears. She must have tasted mine. The taste of tears, at a time like that, is like the taste of a strange wine.

Across her shoulder Spinoza grinned at me from the table. Suddenly I thrust Sally back from me. I began to shake my head. "You'll keep on remembering what a man Spin was! And you should. And I'll never be like him. There was only one Spin!"

"Please!" said Sally. "Please, Amos—"

Pushing her back a little farther, gripping her slim shoulders in my hands, looking into her eyes, eyes hot with tears, I cried, "Look, Sally. You've borne too much. You can't afford to take a chance on a guy like me again. Maybe I'm not an alcoholic. But I was one terrible, idiotic drunk! There are weaknesses in me, honey. I'm loaded with 'em. I might let you down again. Don't gamble on me! You've had enough. I'll never let you chance it!"

She pulled away from me, staring. "You mean—?"

"I mean I'm going away, Sally. I don't know where. I've got to finish a big battle with myself. If I make it, by the help of God, I'll be back—if you're still waiting."

"Amos! I've *already* waited. I've waited and waited—"

"I know. And all I can do is say again how sorry I am. Until I *prove* to you—and to me—that I mean what I say. I can only hope, and pray, that you won't get tired of waiting longer—to see if I'm a *man!*"

"Listen to me, Amos—"

"Don't say anything more. Please. You see, I'm not sure of myself, whether or not I *will* be a man! I've just got to go and find out. So hang on and pray for me, darling. Pray hard!"

I whirled and fled through the door.

CHAPTER 21

I DROVE BACK to Spinoza's place.

I passed two taverns on the way. And a feeling was growing bigger and bigger in me: I would be passing a lot of taverns in the days to come. Somewhere in me a song stirred, one that Spinoza used to sing:

> *A charge to keep I have,*
> *A God to glorify. . . .*

In a day or so we would hold Spinoza's funeral. I'd stay for that. Then where? In my heart I knew that Spinoza would want me to stay and help carry on the work he had planned.

I was standing in the room with my eyes shut, praying, without trying to pray, when suddenly an awesome joy was running through me. I lifted my head and said aloud, "I will not lose! I've got help!"

It was a new world that I was in. I knew it. Don't ask me *how* I knew. Let life have a few mysteries, man! Let God do His thing without asking too many questions! Call it a miracle. Call it what you like. It doesn't matter. What matters is that I had begun to *live!*

A knock on the door broke in on my ecstasy.

When I opened the door there stood Sally. Before I could say anything she said, "Amos, did you think that I was bluffing, all these years?"

"Bluffing?" I stood staring at her.

"I'm a Christian, darling!"

I nodded. "Of course. Even a saint—like Spinoza!"

"Christian people forgive others. Even their enemies. What about forgiving those they love?"

I spread out my hands. I said, "Sally—"

"Hasn't the Lord said that if we confess Him before men we shall be confessed before the angels of heaven?"

"Well, I suppose so—"

"Let me tell you something, Amos. After you left I prayed more earnestly than I've prayed for a long time. I feel God has answered me. He doesn't want me to run out on you right when you need me most! So you just forget about the past. We begin *now!* God will see that you come through. I feel it. I *know* it!"

"I just don't want to hurt you ever again, Sally."

"Never mind. Just stop this silly talk about running off somewhere to see if you're going to be a man! You will prove you're a man—right here, while I watch you do it! I've waited too long for you to come back to let you go again now!"

Her eyes were clear; they were beautiful. For an instant a thought caught on my mind: Marilyn Hunter, in all her sophisticated lifetime, would never know that there *were* such women in the world as Sally Gann!

"Come on, darling," said Sally. "Let's go home."

I caught her in my arms, holding her hard to me, my heart hammering and singing. Spinoza Jones's ghost probably influenced my next words.

"Like, lovely woman, I'm home already! Home with you—and with God!"